GEORGE MEETS HIS MATCH

KRISTIN BAUER GANOUNG

Illustrated by
K. E. GADEKEN

Prairieland Press

Published by Prairieland Press
PO Box 2404
Fremont, NE 68026-2404
Printed in the U.S.A.

Publisher's Cataloging-in-Publication data

Names: Ganoung, Kristin Bauer, author. | Gadekan, K.E., illustrator.
Title: George meets his match / Kristin Bauer Ganoung ; illustrated by K. E. Gadeken.
Series: George Series
Description: Fremont, NE: Prairieland Press, 2021. | Summary: Farm cat George is accidentally trapped
at the local library and must cooperate with the other library pets in order to return home.
Identifiers: LCCN: 2020920589 | ISBN: 978-1-944132-38-5 (Hardcover) | 978-1-944132-39-2 (pbk.) |
978-1-944132-40-8 (ebook)
Subjects: LCSH Cats--Juvenile fiction. | Doppelgängers--Juvenile fiction. | Friendship--Juvenile fiction. |
Domestic animals--Juvenile fiction. | CYAC Cats--Fiction. | Doppelgängers--Fiction. | Friendship--
Fiction. | Domestic animals--Fiction. | BISAC JUVENILE FICTION / General | JUVENILE FICTION /
Animals / Cats
Classification: LCC PZ7.1.G363 Ge 2021 | DDC [Fic]--dc23

Prairieland Press™

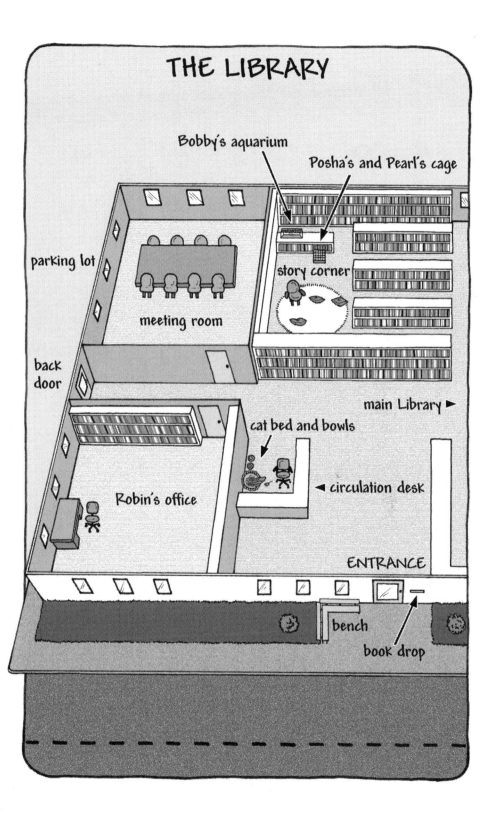

THE LIBRARY

Bobby's aquarium

Posha's and Pearl's cage

parking lot

story corner

meeting room

back door

main Library ▶

cat bed and bowls

Robin's office

◀ circulation desk

ENTRANCE

bench

book drop

Become a
Member of the Club!

Join the Prairieland Press Readers' Club and be one of the first to hear about our special discount offers and new books from our authors.

Visit our website today!
www.prairielandpress.com

In loving memory of my uncle,
Dr. Donald P. Dreyer, a veterinarian
whom even George would have loved.

CONTENTS

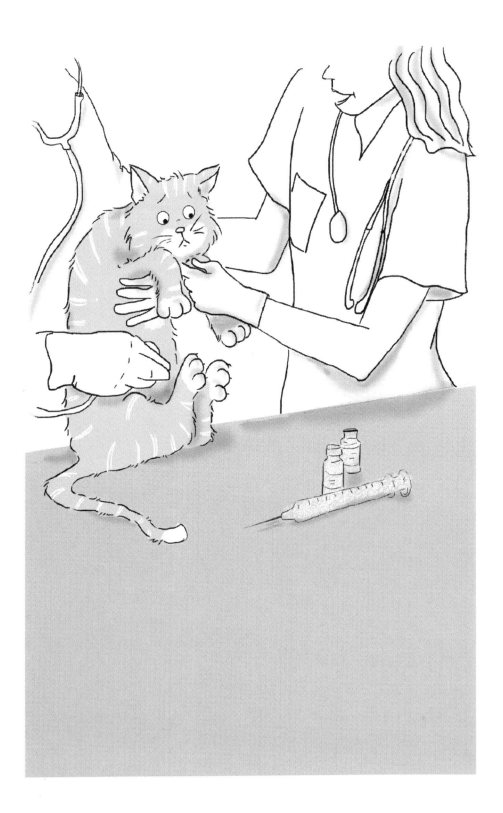

THE VET

Don't let him touch me!

I wished my human, Emma, would listen better. She was obviously leaving me to the mercy of this strange, white-jacketed fellow she called The Vet. *Me,* her feline chief in charge of security, the most necessary animal on her farm.

My tail poofed and I tried to claw my way off the table where Emma had put me, but another human, The Vet's assistant, was holding me down. She was petting me, pretending to be friendly, but I wasn't fooled. The howling and barking I could hear from some other room in this strange place made it clear that I wasn't The Vet's only victim. Besides that, some sharp, medicine-y smell was clogging my nose, making me want to sneeze and choke at the same time.

All I wanted to do was escape. Unfortunately, my claws weren't making much headway on the slippery metal tabletop. *Don't leave me here, Emma,* I yowled. *This guy has a crazy look in his eye.*

"George, calm down. You'll be fine. Dr. Ryder will fix your broken leg and you'll be good as new." Emma was petting me, too, but I was too busy trying to scrabble my way back into her arms to enjoy it.

The Assistant had me in a death grip while The Vet walked toward me with a pointy thing that reminded me of an extra long cactus spine. Whatever he was going to do, it looked like it would hurt. "Don't worry, George. We'll have you back in business in no time," he said in his fakey-nice voice. Then he jabbed the pointy thing into my hip.

YEEEOOOOWWWW! I managed to rake a set of claws in his direction to let him know that I didn't believe him one bit. He jerked backwards, out of range, but at least he took the pointy thing away.

The Assistant loosened her grip and I could hear freedom calling. I got ready to spring off the table and make a run for the door—but my legs weren't cooperating. They were going all wobbly. A heavy weight seemed to be pressing against my eyelids, and I couldn't think straight.

I could hear Emma's voice from the distance. "I've got to go, George, but I'll be back to pick you up soon. You'll be good as new."

Emma leaving? But somehow I didn't have the energy

2

to be worried about her abandoning me. I gave a huge yawn. A nap. That's what I needed. I'd fake a nap, then escape when the humans were looking the other way. As my legs crumpled underneath me, I laid my head against the cool, slick metal and closed my eyes.

Just a little snooze. Just to fool the humans. Nothing more than a quick catnap. Then I'd be on my way.

And I drifted off to dreamland.

* * *

Unfortunately, dreamland wasn't very fun, either. My coyote nemesis, Old Mangy, was there, and I was forced to replay our fight from earlier in the day. He'd tried to break into the chicken pen to gobble up the baby chicks. My duckling deputy, Kid, had helped me round up the chicks and get them safely out of the way. Then I distracted Old Mangy while my two doggy companions, Festus and Brutus, locked the coyote—and me—in the pen. That'd kept everyone safe—except me, of course.

Old Mangy had threatened to eat me, so I'd had to do some fast talking to convince him that we could make a deal: the dogs would let him out of the pen if he'd let me live, and they'd also let him have a snack out of their food bowls every once in a while so he wouldn't need to stalk the farm animals anymore.

The mention of free food had done the trick, and Old Mangy had agreed. But not before giving me a good chomp on the leg. Which was why I was here at this torture chamber called The Vet's.

The Vet's? My dream world was so real I could almost smell the place again—the scents of wet fur, dog drool, and medicine all competing for my attention.

I sneezed and opened my eyes. There was nothing familiar about the gray wall I was staring at nor the soft pad I was lying on, but the smell was definitely the same. Great. I wasn't just dreaming about The Vet's. I was still here—but now there were no humans in sight.

I tried to stand, but my injured front leg felt stiff as a stick. It was wrapped in something that looked like one of Emma's white socks but wasn't nearly as soft. My back legs weren't cooperating, either. I ended up flopping back onto my side.

I narrowed my eyes and tried again. And flopped again.

"Won't do much good, mate," said a cheerful voice. "Just relax and wait a bit."

I tried to focus in the general direction of the voice, but my eyes kept going crossed. I seemed to be staring at a set of bars, like I was in a cage or something. A small black dog—or maybe it was two small black dogs, my eyes couldn't decide—was peering through another set of bars across an aisle from me.

"What?" I tried to say. But the word came out more like "Uhh."

The pooch must've known what I meant, though. He

cocked his head. "It's just the medicine wearing off, old boy. Saw it with your twin beside you, too, only he woke up a bit quicker than you."

Twin? "I don't know what you're talking about," I tried to say. But "Duh nuh wuh," was what I heard coming out of my mouth.

The black pooch sat and scratched an ear with a back paw. "Don't know what you're saying, but we can talk later. When you're feeling a wee bit better." Then he circled several times on his stubby legs and settled in a corner. My eyes cleared enough for me to realize that he was in a cage, too, directly opposite mine. I thought about turning my head to check for this "twin" he'd mentioned, but my neck muscles were wobbling and I was still feeling light-headed and cross-eyed. I decided I needed more sleep.

So I sprawled onto the cage floor and returned to my dreams.

2

KIDNAPPED

I was awakened by the sound of kids' voices. At first I figured Emma's niece and nephew had come for a visit and were getting ready to stuff me into one of those pink dresses that the little girl seemed to like so much. I went into automatic poof.

But then my eyes settled on the source of the noise. Two kids I'd never seen before were peering into the cage next to mine.

"Don't touch!" a human voice warned from somewhere out of my sight. It sounded like The Vet.

The boy shoved his hands into his pockets. "Yeah, Dad, we know. We're just looking."

The girl turned to stare into my cage, then poked a finger inside. "Do you suppose they're brothers?" she asked.

The boy pulled her back. "Keep your fingers out or he might bite."

"But I wanna know if they're brothers."

The boy squinted at a white tag clipped to the side of my cage then looked over at the cage next to mine.

I looked, too. My muscles were cooperating better now, but not well enough to keep my jaw from dropping open when I saw the occupant of the neighboring cage. It was a cat. An orange cat. And he looked *exactly* like me, right down to the same white sock-like thing on one of his front legs.

"Dunno," the boy said, interrupting my shock. "But probably not. They've got different names and different owners. Come on. Let's go outside and look at the horse." He turned and headed for the door, probably expecting her to follow.

Instead, she stuck out her tongue at him and put her fingers into my cage again. Even with a set of bars between us, I wasn't taking any chances. I swiped at her with my claws.

My aim was off—still feeling a little uncoordinated— but it was worth the effort. She snatched back her hand so fast that her fingers almost got tangled in the bars. The cage jiggled, and the white tag fell off and landed on the floor with a *plop*.

"Jessie, come *on*," the boy said, frowning. Good for him. Get her away from me.

She stuck out her tongue at *me* this time and swaggered

away like she wasn't afraid of me at all. Her shoulder brushed against the cage next to mine, and there was another jiggle and *plop* as the tag on the other orange cat's cage also fell.

The boy stomped back. "*Jess.* You're going to get us both in trouble." He grabbed the tags off the floor and studied them. Then he clipped one of them on my cage and the other on the cage next to mine. Finally, he grabbed hold of the girl's hand and pulled her out of the door.

I breathed a sigh of relief and began licking my poofed fur. It's a little hard to look professional when behind bars, but I wanted to give it my best shot. I turned to the orange cat in the cage next to mine. "Hi," I said. "My name's George and I'm chief in charge of security on the farm where I live. How about you?"

The other cat was grooming himself, too, and gave me a wary eye. Maybe he thought I looked dangerous.

"No need to be worried." I tilted my head. "Unless you're a mouse or a rat, that is." I laughed, but the other cat didn't. What was wrong with this guy?

"I don't talk to strangers." He quickly scooted into the far back corner of his cage and curled into a tight ball, turning his back toward me and covering his face with his tail so that only the tips of his ears were still showing through the mound of orange fur.

Fine. Let him be that way. When Emma got here to pick me up, I'd never see him again. *If* Emma ever came.

I looked around. The black pooch who'd talked with me before was gone. The only critters left in this jail were the other orange cat and me. I stood and began pacing—uh, hobbling—the length of the cage. My muscles were cooperating again, but my wrapped front leg was being more contrary than Felix at his worst.

Felix, in case you didn't know, is a stubborn gray cat who recently moved to the farm with his humans, Jason and Lil. He asked me to teach him to catch mice, but argued with me constantly. The only useful thing he'd done lately was to alert Emma to the fight going on between Old Mangy and me in the chicken pen. Emma made Old Mangy scram for sure, but then she'd noticed my injured leg. And that was why I was stuck in this tiny cage, hardly able to walk.

I couldn't let my uncooperative leg be an excuse for sitting around, though. I really needed to get back to the farm. Felix was notorious for disappearing into the house and leaving the work for someone else to do, and I didn't want my deputy, Kid, to be taking on any bad guys by herself. The duckling had plenty of spunk, but she lacked some important self-defense features, like sharp teeth and fine-tuned coordination.

Suddenly I heard a door opening. Maybe the kids were coming back. I stood and rubbed against the bars, hoping to look cute and fluffy enough that they might open my cage and let me out. But the two incoming humans were The Assistant with the fingers of steel and another lady I'd never seen before. The Stranger had dark hair, cropped and curly like the sheep during the summer when their wool is growing back after shearing. A pair of glasses dangled on a string around her neck, and she was holding a purple pet carrier.

I humphed and sat down to bathe my good front leg. I didn't need to watch them since they were clearly here to pick up the other feline inmate.

The Assistant stopped in front of my cage and examined the tag. "Here we are. All fixed up and ready to go."

What? I stopped in mid lick and looked at both of the humans again. Ready to go where? Surely Emma wouldn't send a stranger to fetch me. Or would she?

The dark-haired lady peered through the bars. Then she set the glasses on her nose and studied me more closely. "Goodness. Here I'd been thinking it was Briggston's left leg that was injured."

The Assistant picked up the tag and studied it again. "This is definitely Briggston. Probably both legs were bruised in the accident, but the right leg was injured the worst. Just keep it wrapped for about a week so that he's forced to stay off of it."

I decided to return to my grooming. Surely if I ignored them, they'd figure out I wasn't Briggston and leave.

"You ready to go home, Briggs?" The Stranger still had her glasses on and was watching me.

I turned my back and concentrated on smoothing my tail, which was poofing just a little.

"You're not still mad, are you, kitty?"

Kitty? My tail poofed even more.

"You learned your lesson the hard way, for sure, not to take a nap right behind me when I'm standing at the circulation desk. You're lucky I didn't hurt you even worse when I backed up and trampled you with these big feet of mine."

I glared at her and hissed to make my meaning clear: Go away. I'm not your cat. Take that crazy critter in the cage next to me. I glanced over at the other orange cat, but he was still tucked in a tight ball, sleeping. He definitely needed to wake up so he could set his human straight. I tried to squeeze my paw into his cage to give him a jab, but it wouldn't fit.

While I was concentrating on getting his attention, The Assistant opened my cage and hefted me out. I unsheathed my claws, prepared to defend myself. But she was fast. She stuffed me into the pet carrier before I was able to do any damage.

The wire door quickly snapped shut, and I felt myself being lifted off the ground. All I could see through the skinny slits on the carrier's side were the ladies' feet. "Sorry about that," The Stranger said, her voice coming from above me. "He's not usually this cranky."

"Don't worry about it. I'd be cranky, too, if my leg was hurting that badly," The Assistant said.

"I suppose you're right." Another jerk on the carrier.

"Guess you've earned the right to a bad attitude, Briggston. Time to go home."

Home? I doubted it. I was being kidnapped! Catnapped! Carted off against my will!

I started yowling, hoping that if I was loud enough, the real Briggston would wake up and save me.

"Briggston!" I heard from overhead. The pet carrier started moving toward the door. I upped the volume of my caterwauling, but the real Briggston didn't stir until I was almost across the room.

I saw his eyes go wide—then the door thudded shut between us.

The Vet was standing in the next room. "Bye-bye, Briggston." He waved as I whooshed by.

I yowled even louder. Put me down! I'm not your cat!

It didn't do any good, though. Humans are notorious for not understanding simple cat language. Before I knew it, I was in the back seat of a car. The Stranger climbed into the front and started the engine.

Wherever we were going, I was sure it wasn't home. I screeched my outrage the entire way.

3

PRISONER

When the car finally stopped and The Stranger lifted out the carrier, I could see that we were still in town, in a large open space with lots of other cars. No tractors or farm trucks in sight.

We headed for a building that didn't look like any place I'd seen before. It was made of red bricks, like Emma's house, but was *way* bigger. It was tall enough to be two houses stacked on top of each other. And there wasn't a yard with a fence, either. Just a strip of grass running along the sidewalk. I was almost curious enough to stop yowling and look more closely.

But on the other paw, I *had* to get back home. So I kept yowling.

"Hush up, Briggs." The Stranger peered at me

through the carrier's little wire door. "I can't take you inside if you're hollering like that."

I screeched even louder.

She frowned. "What has gotten into you, cat? Guess we'll have to go in the back way, so we don't cause a huge disruption."

But a disruption was what I wanted. People staring, shouting, opening the carrier and letting me go!

Once inside, The Stranger carried me to a small square room at the end of a long hallway. A strange-looking table with drawers stood in one corner of the room, and two of the walls had shelves that were packed with books. I hadn't seen books since my kittenhood, when I lived with Emma's sister, Twila, in town. Twila would sometimes leave books on the kitchen table, but we kittens weren't allowed on the table so I was never able to examine one closely. The Stranger had a *lot* more books than Twila ever had, though.

"I don't like having you in my office," The Stranger said, as she set the carrier on the floor. "But I guess I have no choice. I'll never hear the end of it if I let you out into the main part of the library acting like *that*." She opened the carrier. "Come on, Briggs. Be a good boy."

She crouched down and held out her hand like she was offering to pet me.

But I wasn't in any mood to make friends. I hissed at her.

She sighed. "Fine. I'll go get your things, and you can stay in here until you've calmed down."

She left, but I stayed in the carrier. For all I knew, this was a trick to get me to come out. I didn't want the carrier to disappear. I wanted her to take me right back to The Vet, where Emma would be able to find me!

When she got back, she said, "That medicine has made you go completely loopy, Briggs, but I think I know how to fix your bad attitude."

There was the sound of a can opening from somewhere above me and then an incredibly yummy, fishy smell. A few tail twitches later, The Stranger returned with a bowl in her hand, which she put down just outside the carrier door.

"Here you go, Briggs. Your favorite: tuna."

Tuna. Couldn't recall Emma ever serving up something fancy like that, although I'd had fish from Ted's pond after he took his nephew fishing. Fish was a special treat. And now fish was being delivered right to my front door—well, to the front of the carrier, at least. I was going to have to step out to get it, though.

I hesitated, wondering if this was a ploy so The Stranger could whisk away the carrier the moment I did. But the scent of tuna was wafting toward me, curling around my nose, and making my stomach rumble. It'd been a long time since my last meal—clear back this morning before my battle with Old Mangy. Besides, this might be a once-in-a-lifetime opportunity to taste tuna.

Maybe I could eat while sitting right next to the carrier. If The Stranger decided to grab it, I could jump back inside.

I slunk forward on my belly, inch by inch, watching The Stranger very carefully. She was watching me, too, but wasn't making any sudden moves. When I reached the bowl, I poked my nose inside, keeping one eye on her just in case. She put her hands on her hips, and I jumped, but she stayed where she was. I snarfed down the tuna in nothing flat and scrubbed the bowl clean with my tongue.

Yum, yum. Too bad Emma didn't serve food like that. It was the best-tasting supper I'd had in a long time.

The Stranger smiled, then turned and left the room, shutting the door firmly behind her.

Well, what should I do now? More yowling? My throat was feeling pretty scratchy from the previous go-round. I might have to save the yowling till after I'd had a drink of water. I slunk all the way out of the carrier and looked around. Two cat bowls, which I assumed belonged to Briggston, sat on the floor near the far wall.

I cocked my head to listen. Couldn't hear any footsteps. Maybe The Stranger was leaving me alone for now. I limped cautiously toward the bowls, stopped to listen again, then took a few more steps. Eventually I made it across the room and poked my nose into one of the bowls. Kibbles—the tasty, crunchy kind that Lil gets for Felix, who's spoiled rotten. Since Briggston wasn't around to eat them, I helped myself.

The other bowl had water, thank goodness. I lapped

up about half of it, then cocked my head and listened again. Still no footsteps. Might as well do a little exploring while I had the chance.

I didn't have to look far to find Briggston's bed. A basket sat on the floor not far from the bowls. Inside was a fluffy purple blanket. Wow. Briggston's bed looked so comfortable!

I patted the blanket with my good paw. Oooh, it was soft. I listened for The Stranger again. Still no footsteps. I might as well try out the bed. I'd leave a few cat hairs and my scent for Briggston to enjoy when he got home.

I climbed in, tucked myself into a ball with my stick leg stretched under my head like a pillow, and sighed. This felt SO good. The last couple of hours had been exhausting. I definitely needed a nap. If I kept an ear out for footsteps like I kept an ear out for mice when I took a snooze on the farm, I could be up and back in the carrier the moment The Stranger opened the door.

No worries.

And I fell asleep.

TRICKED

When I woke from my nap, the room was getting a little shadowy, which meant it was probably getting dark outside. Guess the trauma of the day must've made me more tired than I thought. I was long overdue for going home. Kid would be getting worried and Felix would forget to do the evening report with Pauline, the llama in charge of sheep security on my farm. I couldn't have Pauline threatening to resign again.

I was limping back to the carrier when I realized it had disappeared! How had that happened? I'd been listening so carefully!

I'm not proud to admit that at that moment, I got a little panicky. My fur went all tingly and my whiskers went *sprong*, straight from my cheeks like porcupine quills. I hobbled all over the office, hoping I'd just overlooked the purple carrier, but my mind was doing jumpy, twitchy things. Instead of finding anything, I ended up bouncing off a set of legs that appeared from nowhere in front of me.

A pair of arms reached down and scooped me up. "Briggston, calm down, you crazy cat."

My fur poofed and my back claws scrabbled at thin air, but The Stranger didn't seem to notice. She gave my head a pat. "Let's go over to my desk and sit for a minute." And she carried me, kicking and squirming, across the room.

She put me on top of her desk and I went into a crouch. Stick leg or not, I was ready to jump down and run. But then she pulled out a couple of things from a drawer: a purple, cloth-covered mouse and a kitty treat. I froze. The mouse was obviously not real, but it sure smelled interesting. And the kitty treat—well, Emma *never* gives me kitty treats.

I swiped at the treat, and The Stranger obligingly dropped it on the desk where I could reach it. I kept my eye on her while I crunched it. She didn't move, although the mouse she was holding began to twitch. Surely it wasn't alive, but it was wiggling and jiggling so temptingly.

I batted at it with my good paw, and The Stranger laughed. "Oh, Briggs. You always love your catnip toy."

I had no idea what catnip was, or a toy, either, but the mouse thing was making me feel a little wild and crazy. I swiped at it again, hooking it with my claws and tugging hard enough that it flew out of The Stranger's hand and onto the floor. I teetered on the edge of the desk and looked down, wondering how I could get to it without falling on my nose.

"You need help off the desk, old boy?" The Stranger picked me up and set me onto the floor.

I didn't even bristle at her touch, the toy smelled so good. I tried to ignore my injured front leg and attacked the phony mouse as best I could with my good set of claws. The more I batted at it, the wilder and better I felt. I swatted it across the carpet then galumphed after it on three legs as it flew into the wall. I boxed it in the other direction and pounced on it.

This was living! Kitty treats and toys. I felt positively kittenish again. I hooked my claws into the toy and pulled. Suddenly I heard a loud ripping sound and a dusty, leafy substance sprayed out of the mouse and into my nose. I let out a gigantic sneeze.

The Stranger had been laughing at me, but now she went silent. "Briggston, why did you do that?" she said.

Uh, oh. Something had gone wrong, but I didn't know what. I backed away from the scrap of purple cloth that didn't look mousey anymore. The Stranger walked over and picked it up. "Oh, my," she said.

The crease on her forehead looked a lot like Emma's does right before she gives me a lecture about sitting in her flower bed. I backed away even further.

The Stranger didn't launch into a lecture, though. She examined the toy, looked over at me, and grimaced. "Who would've thought that a visit to the vet would've turned you into such a terror?" She shook her head. "Guess we both need a good night's sleep."

She scooped up the rest of the mouse powder and tossed it and the scraps of purple cloth into a barrel beside her desk. Then she looked down at me and tapped a finger against her chin. "The thing is, can I trust you roaming the stacks tonight?"

Stacks? My ears perked up. I knew what stacks were. I loved Ted's hay stacks. Those piles of hay were great for climbing and jumping, and there were always critters like mice and crickets hiding in the loose hay at the bottom. If this place had stacks, that's where I wanted to be.

I turned on my motor and rubbed against her leg, trying to act charming and persuasive like my good friend, Alice, had taught me. Just thinking about Alice, with her beautiful black fur and trim white-mitten paws, made me purr even louder.

Alice had been at the farm earlier in the day and had helped Felix alert the humans to Old Mangy's attack. I was lucky she'd been there. Alice lives in town, but she visits the farm quite often because her human, Twila, is Emma's sister.

Alice has a real knack for getting humans to know exactly what she wants, which is why she's been teaching me her tricks. The purring and rubbing strategy she'd shown me was sure working on The Stranger right now.

She bent down and gave my head a pat. "That's better. I'm glad you're finally snapping out of it."

Snapping? Not hardly. That's what dogs do when they're unhappy with a human. I was definitely *not* snapping. Not when I was trying to get The Stranger to do me a favor.

She was smiling, though, and still patting me on the head. "Okay, Briggs, you've convinced me. You'll get your freedom. But if I find a single book out of place..." She shook her finger at me.

Books? Why would there be books in her hay stacks? No matter. I wasn't interested in the books. Just the hay and the critters that lived there. I upped the volume of my purring to let her know I understood.

She opened the door for me.

Freedom! Tail high, I sprang for the opening—and fell *splat*, right on my nose. I'd forgotten about my useless leg. I flattened my ears and pulled myself up, hoping that I wasn't showing red under my orange fur.

The Stranger had the good sense not to laugh at me, though. "After you, Briggston," she said, gesturing down the hallway we'd come through earlier. I limped ahead of her until we got to the biggest room I'd ever seen. It might've been as big as the haymow in Emma's barn. Or maybe bigger. It would've been a great place to store a lot of hay, only there was no hay to be seen. Just books. Shelves and shelves of books.

I stopped, frozen in place, hardly noticing as The

Stranger stepped around me. "See you tomorrow morning, Briggs. Behave yourself."

She walked across the huge room, opened a different door off to the side, and left.

Wait! I didn't want to be left alone in this strange place. Where were the hay stacks? Where were the critters? Where was the smell of dried grass, dust, and summer sunshine?

I shuffled after The Stranger as fast as my stick leg would take me. I could still see her as she walked down the sidewalk to her car. Maybe she'd forgotten to shut the door! I limped forward as fast as I could, keeping my eyes firmly fixed on her. Then without warning, my skull slammed against something *really* hard.

My eyes crossed from the force of the blow. I backed up, shaking my head to get rid of the stars floating around in there, and tried to figure out what I'd run into. The Stranger was climbing into her car now. I wanted to run after her, but I wasn't stupid enough to ram my head twice.

I carefully propped myself on my stick leg and patted at the door with my other paw. It felt very solid, cool, and slick. Ah. Glass. I knew all about glass. Emma had glass windows, which was why I could see into her house but not get inside. She didn't have any glass doors, though.

I pressed my nose against that glass and watched as The Stranger's car headed down the street and disappeared, leaving me all alone in this weird building full of books. Books, not hay. Shelves, not corrals. No other animals or humans in sight. Would The Stranger come back? How was I going to get home?

Suddenly, a shrill whistle split the air. All of my fur instantly stood on end.

It was clear that I was not alone after all.

5

RODENTS, RODENTS EVERYWHERE...AND NONE FOR ME TO EAT

I swiveled and almost landed flat on my face again. Stupid leg! I picked myself up and scanned the shadowy room. The place was quiet again—until I heard a soft rustling coming from somewhere behind all those shelves of books.

I hesitated. If I were back in my barn I'd be heading over to check out the situation, but here I didn't know the rules. I didn't know who belonged and who didn't. Like, I didn't know if there were any dangerous, cat-eating dogs around. The whistling hadn't sounded like a dog, but in this strange place, how could I be sure?

My tail twitched. Well, if I really wanted to know, I guess I'd have to go check it out.

I crept in the direction of the noise, curling around several shelves and sneaking under a table or two, all while trying to keep my stick leg from thudding on the floor. I came to a place where four long, low shelves were grouped in a box shape around a big space in the middle, the same as four panels making sides around a stall in the barn. A wide gap had been left between two of the shelves, like an open gate. I slunk along one of those shelves until I reached the gap, then crooked my neck to peer inside.

Lots of giant pillows and little chairs were scattered around the open spot in the middle, and books—even more books than Emma has sheep—were stacked on the shelves. Skinny books and fat books. Books that were tall, small, and all colors of the rainbow.

Hmm. Lots of human stuff, but nothing that looked dangerous. I cautiously stepped into the opening between the shelves. Another whistle split the air and I practically jumped out of my skin. I spun toward the sound and unsheathed my claws for battle.

But nothing stirred.

I crept further into the open space. Nothing suspicious-looking until…

Sitting on the floor beside one of the shelves was a tall, wire cage. Inside the cage was a ramp crisscrossing from the bottom to a landing on another level, then another ramp leading to yet another level. On the floor of the cage was a purple plastic hut, and sitting in front of the hut were two of the fattest rodents I'd ever seen. Too big to be mice, but not big enough to be prairie dogs or gophers.

"Briggston!" one of them squeaked. "Welcome

home!" She put her front paws against the wire of the cage and stood.

Immediately I went into a crouch, my tail going flick, flick, flick. I wasn't hungry after eating all those fancy kibbles from Briggston's bowl, but I was always ready for a good chase.

"Briggs, what are you doing?" The rodent went down on all fours.

Still flicking my tail, I studied both of them. They were round and fat with small floppy ears and round black eyes. The one who'd spoken had brownish-red fur swirling in every direction like it'd just been licked by a slobbery dog. The other one had smooth, sleek fur of the same brown color, but with swatches of white and black on her head.

I inched forward, favoring my injured leg, until I was close enough to stick my other front paw into the cage and bat at the two of them. They sat out of reach, though, not looking worried at all. In fact, they were staring at me like I'd grown giant donkey ears or something. As strange as this day had been, it wouldn't surprise me if that'd really happened. I took my paw out of the cage and slicked it over my ears, but they felt perfectly normal.

"Briggston, get a grip." Smooth Fur said, coming closer and putting her nose through a space between the wire. "What'd that vet guy do to you? Did he trim your claws too close to the quick?"

For some reason, they both started whistling and squeaking like they'd just heard the best joke ever. They stopped and jumped backward, though, when I hooked my claws around the wire and rattled their cage. "Stop that racket before I..." Before what? My paw wouldn't reach them. I looked more closely at the cage. "...before I figure out how to open this door and come in after you."

That shut them up. They stared at me with their beady black eyes.

"You can do that?" Swirly Fur asked.

I nodded, trying to keep any hint of doubt from showing on my face. Back home I'd watched the dogs open gates although I was too short to do it myself. This cage was more my size, though. I figured I could get the door open if I worked at it.

"Then why haven't you done it before?" Both animals were looking strangely excited.

"Because I've never *been* here before," I growled. "I'm George, okay? Not this crazy Briggston fellow everyone thinks I am!"

They went quiet again—for a few flicks of my tail at least—while studying me. "You sure *look* like Briggston," Swirly Fur said.

"Unfortunately." I scowled, then sat down. My injured leg was throbbing. "Our cages were side by side at The Vet's, and somehow The Stranger mistook me for him."

"The Stranger?" Smooth Fur said, tilting her head. "Who's that?"

"The lady who brought me here."

For some reason, the rodents started whistling and chortling again.

"What's so funny?" I asked.

"Her name's Robin," Swirly Fur said, "not The Stranger."

"Robin?" I narrowed my eyes. "She's not a bird."

If rodents had shoulders, these two would've shrugged theirs. "That's her name," Swirly Fur said. "Dunno why."

"We need to introduce ourselves." Smooth Fur poked her nose through the wires. "I'm Posha and this is my sister, Pearl."

Posha and Pearl? "What's with the fancy names?"

Smooth—I mean, Posha—tilted her nose in the air. "Every library animal is named by the kids who come to story time. We guinea pigs have fancy names since the kids dress us up like actresses for—"

"Wait a minute." I hooked a paw on the cage, and Posha scooted backward. "What did you say you were?"

"Uh." She scratched her ear. "I said, 'We guinea pigs—'"

"Yeah, that. You're a guinea pig? I thought you were some sort of rat."

Posha's jaw dropped. "A rat? Well, I never!" She spun around, displaying her round backside. "Do you see a tail?"

"Uh, no."

"That's because guinea pigs do *not* have tails. We're much better looking than common *rats*, after all." Posha stuck her nose into the air and waddled inside the purple hut with Pearl tailing—uh, following—her.

Maybe I'd offended them, but that was okay. I wasn't in the mood to talk with a couple of tailless rats anyway. I was tired, my injured leg felt like it was on fire, and my entire body was begging for a nap.

I started hobbling over to a big pillow lying conveniently close by when suddenly I heard a slithering, rustling sound coming from somewhere above me. I shot straight in the air, landed on my nose—again—and scrambled to my feet to meet this surprise attack.

At first I didn't see anything suspicious. I scanned the shelves carefully, peering up one, two, then three levels until I spotted a large glass box sitting on the top shelf. And inside the box, staring back at me was—a snake! I flattened my ears and hissed. I wasn't afraid of snakes, mind you, but I sure didn't trust any critter who'd surprise me like that.

The snake was staring at me with his head raised and his tongue flicking. "You're being ssssuper brave tonight, Briggsssston," he said.

My whiskers bristled. I swiped in his direction with a set of claws even though I was too far away to hook anything but air. "I'm not Briggston, okay? I AM NOT Briggston!"

The snake didn't even flinch. "Okay," he said. "Sssso who are you?"

"George!" I yelled. "My name is George. You all

remember that!" And I bumbled my way over to the nearest pillow, laid down and wrapped my tail around me as tightly as I could. *This is only a nightmare,* I told myself, squinching my eyes shut. *When I wake up in the morning, I'll be back home where I belong.*

I could only hope.

LIBRARY LOCKUP

No such luck. When I woke in the morning, I was firmly planted on the same pillow, lying in a bright puddle of sunlight. Not a bad way to start the day—unless you've been locked up in a strange place surrounded by even stranger critters.

I yawned, stood and stretched, then looked around. By putting my paws on a shelf and standing on my tiptoes, I could see the snake in his glass box. He was mostly hidden under a hollowed-out log, but the end of his tail was sticking out. It was a yellowish color with brown blotches. Bull snake, I figured. I'd seen one or two of them in the pasture on the farm. Emma doesn't like me to harass them because she says they keep the rodent population from exploding.

Now that I was gone, she'd find out who the real

rodent exterminator was. I needed to get back home before the mice completely took over. I limped back to my pillow and gave myself a lick-down. My fur had poofed so much yesterday I was afraid it might freeze in that position.

While I was bathing, the glass door to the library opened and The Stranger—that is, Robin—came in. She put her bags down on a tall table across from the door and walked over to where I was sitting.

"Good morning, Briggston," she said. "I'm surprised to find you here in the story corner instead of in your basket. You seem to be behaving yourself, though." She gave me a pat on the head before going over to the snake's glass box. "Good morning, Bobby Scales. Did you sleep well?"

The snake didn't move, which didn't seem to surprise Robin. She was already heading to the guinea pigs' cage. "Good morning, Posha. Good morning, Pearl."

The two guinea pigs scuttled out of their hut and ran around in circles, squeaking and whistling as loud as the back-up beeper on Ted's loader tractor.

"Yup. Breakfast coming up." Robin opened their cage and started scooping pellets into their dish from a container sitting on the shelf nearby. "You need to be ready for story time this afternoon. We're going to be talking about the contest, you know."

I didn't know what story time was—or a contest either —but I was certainly acquainted with breakfast. I stumbled off the pillow and rubbed against Robin's leg. Not that I wanted to be friendly, but I needed breakfast too. I'm always able to think better on a full stomach, and I definitely needed to plan how to get out of this place.

"Glad you're feeling better, Briggs. I'll go get your bowls and move them back behind the circulation desk where they belong." She gave me a pat and started walking away.

I had no idea what a circulation desk might be. Emma sometimes talked about air circulation in the barn. That's why she leaves the barn door open on summer evenings when she milks. I always figured that meant she wanted the outside air to be moving in. Could the circulation desk move, too? This I had to see.

I trailed Robin while she fetched the food and water dishes and kept following as she brought the bowls back out to the big room. My ears shot up as she went behind that same tall table where she'd piled her bags. Was that the circulation desk?

Robin set the bowls in the corner by the wall, but I stopped and studied the situation. The desk was big and looked like two tables pushed together to make a corner. One of the tables was attached to the library's brick wall to make a second corner. The desk wasn't open underneath like tables, though. Instead, its front was covered with a solid panel of wood. It looked too big and heavy to move, no matter what Robin said. I decided I'd keep an eye on it—while having my breakfast, of course.

35

As I crunched my kibbles, Robin shuffled things around on top of the desk. I'd finished my breakfast and was cleaning my whiskers when another lady came in through the back hallway. She had pink hair pulled back in a ponytail and big, dangly rings hanging from each ear. I froze. Emma's niece likes to wear pink, and she'd forced me to wear a pink princess dress once. Since then, I didn't trust anyone wearing pink.

The pink lady gave me a smile. "Good to see you back, Briggston," she said, as she joined Robin behind the circulation desk.

"Good morning, Celia," Robin said. "Ready for another day?"

"Ready-freddy," Celia said. "Bring them on."

Robin left the circulation desk and crossed over to the big glass door where I'd rammed my head last night. This was my chance. All I had to do was slip outside, hide until the humans got tired of looking for me, then wander up and down sidewalks until I recognized something. I was pretty sure that this was the town where my friend, Alice, lived, and I knew that if I could find her, she'd take me to Twila, who'd take me home to Emma. Twila had done that the last time I was lost.

I tried to creep along behind Robin without being seen, figuring I'd need to be close to the door to slip out when it opened. With my injured leg, though, I couldn't move very fast.

"You have someone on your tail, Robin."

Rats! I'd forgotten Celia might be watching. Evidently Robin didn't realize that she didn't *have* a tail because she turned around and looked down…there I was.

"Briggston, what are you doing?" Robin turned a little knob on the glass door but kept her eyes on me. "Are you trying to get out? Was your visit to the vet enough of an adventure that you want to see more of the world?" She smiled one of those goofy smiles, like Emma does when we're in the garden together and she asks if I'd like one of the carrots she's just pulled. *Yech.*

Celia piped up. "I still think it'd be a good idea to put a sign on the door so that people will watch out for him. I've said that before."

Robin frowned. "But Briggston's never been interested in getting out."

Celia shrugged. "You said he's been acting strange."

"Hmmm." Robin narrowed her eyes. "You're probably right."

I stood by the door, hoping she was going to open it, but instead she went to the desk, did some sort of clickety-click thing with her fingers while she stared at a big box sitting up there, and came back with a piece of paper, which she attached to the door.

"That takes care of that," she said, swiping her hands together. "You don't like being outside anyway, remember, Briggs?"

Maybe the real Briggston didn't, but this wasn't Briggston she was dealing with. I decided to keep my eye on the door from behind a nearby book shelf. Someone would surely open it.

And I was right. Lots of humans came into the library while I sat there. But they all looked at the paper Robin had put on the door and then spotted me staggering toward them with my leg wrapped like a caterpillar trussed up in a cocoon. After several failed escape attempts, I realized I just wasn't fast enough. I stumped back to where the other animals were. Maybe they could give me some advice on how to break out of here.

When I got there, though, the corner was full of kids. I was about to turn tail and find a quieter spot when one of them saw me. "Briggston!" she squealed. And before I could get away, she scooped me up and carried me, feet dragging on the floor, over to where a bunch of other kids were seated. I thought about hooking her with my claws—just to encourage her to put me down—but with everyone staring, I figured it wasn't a good idea.

She plunked down onto a pillow, still clutching me around my middle. "We're reading *Puss in Boots* for story time today, Briggston. You're going to love it!"

I didn't know what story time was, but her lap was comfortable and I was getting tired of stumping around on three legs. I decided to stay and figure out what everyone was doing.

Looking around, I saw a couple of other kids holding Posha and Pearl, and a boy who had Bobby Scales in his lap. I didn't know humans ever touched snakes. Even Emma, who claimed to like snakes, never picked one up.

"Don't look at the snake, Briggston," the girl said, and turned so that she was blocking my view of the reptile. Weird. Maybe he wasn't supposed to be out of his cage.

Celia didn't seem to mind, though. She was sitting in front of the group holding a book and completely ignoring the snake. When she opened the book, I could see a cat inside. A very flat cat. I couldn't understand how a cat could be so flat—unless it got that way by being shut inside the book. It wasn't a normal cat, either, as it was wearing human boots and a hat. Maybe some kid had dressed him that way, just like Emma's niece had done to me.

My eyes narrowed. Maybe that's what story time was —a time to stuff animals into clothes and shut them flat in a book. I unsheathed my claws and got ready to scramble off the girl's lap, but then Celia started talking. Then she turned a page and talked some more.

As she kept turning pages and talking, the kids were all leaning forward, listening intently. I didn't seem to be in imminent danger of being stuffed in a princess dress—or boots, either. So I decided to stay a little longer. I liked the sound of Celia's voice. It had a sing-song rhythm that made my eyes droop.

Surely a little nap wouldn't hurt. I'd keep my ears tuned for trouble. Nothing strange could possibly happen while I enjoyed a few Z's. Right?

7

A SNEAKY ENTRANCE

I was having a strange dream. Felix was on mouse patrol with me, dressed up in Ted's big boots which clunked so loudly that the mice could hear us coming from clear across the farmyard. Suddenly the clunking stopped. I jerked awake to discover that Celia was no longer talking. Robin had joined the group and was holding up a piece of paper with flattened Posha and Pearl staring out at us, dressed like pink princesses. While I'd been napping, the guinea pigs must have been stuck into human clothes and flattened, just like the cat in the book!

My fur instantly poofed, and I scrambled off the girl's lap, intent on making a run for it so the humans couldn't do the same to me. I was so busy watching behind me, though, that I blundered smack into another kid. I looked around...

…and there was Posha, sitting in the kid's lap just like before. Confused, I looked back at Robin. She was still holding the paper with flat Posha and Pearl. How could there be two Poshas?

Before I could ask what was going on, the girl who'd been holding me grabbed me again. "Listen up, Briggston," she said. "Maybe *you* can enter the contest this year."

Contest? What was a contest?

"…the Best Dressed Pet contest at the fair just like last year," Robin was saying. She held up a frilly purple ribbon. "The guinea pigs won grand champion last year for their princess costumes!"

The kids all clapped and cheered.

Robin held up her hand, and the kids quieted down. "So we need to choose their costumes for this year."

"Pirates!" one of the boys called out.

One of the girls squealed. "No, cheerleaders!"

The group erupted as kids started waving their hands and jumping up and down. "Pirates!" "Cowboys!" "Clowns!"

I laid my ears flat and gathered myself to run, but Robin held up her hand again and the kids hushed. "Okay, we'll make this fun," she said. "If you have an idea for what the guinea pigs should wear, you create the costumes and bring them to the library. We'll take pictures of the guinea pigs in the different costumes. The contest is on Tuesday, one week from today. At story time on

Monday, we'll look at the pictures and vote for the best costume."

The girl who was holding me raised her hand. "Can we dress Briggston and Bobby Scales for the contest, too?"

Instantly my whiskers bristled and I tensed, preparing to hightail it out of there. Robin looked at me. "I don't think so, Britney. Not this year. Briggston hasn't been feeling too well lately, and we don't want him to hurt his leg again. Besides, you know he doesn't get along very well with Bobby."

The girl, Britney, squeezed me so tight I could barely breath. "Poor Briggston," she said. "Maybe next year. Then you can win a purple ribbon, too."

Before I knew it, she was tugging me off the pillow and toward a shelf. "My turn to read, Briggston. What do you want to hear?"

What did I want to hear? Someone calling me George and telling me they'd take me back to the farm.

The kid pulled a book off the shelf and began flipping through it, pointing to this and that. I was shocked. This book not only had flat cats, but also flat cows, horses, and chickens. None of them was moving or making a sound. I decided I'd better make tracks, or I'd be stuffed in one of these books too.

I tumbled off the kid's lap and hobbled as fast as I could toward the circulation desk where Robin was working. She hadn't tried stuffing me in a book yet. She'd probably keep me safe.

I spent the rest of the afternoon either watching humans or snoozing in Briggston's cat bed, which Robin had brought from her office and put beside the food and water bowls. It was a dreadfully dull way to spend the day —and I was still no closer to figuring out how to get home.

After the kids had cleared out of the library, I decided it might be safe to explore again. I *had* to get back home. The farm was probably falling apart without me.

It didn't take me long to conclude that this place was more escape-proof than Emma's chicken pen. No doors or gaps big enough for even a cricket to squeeze through. I sat by the glass door and stared at the world outside. A strip of green grass waited to be rolled in, a sparrow in a nearby bush begged to be chased, a puddle of sun on the bench outside the door invited me over for a nap. And all of these things were out of my reach.

I took out my frustration by clawing the mat in front of the door.

"Briggston, stop that!" Robin passed me on the way to a book shelf and gave me a squinty frown.

Fine. I glared out the door some more. The sparrow fluttered to the bench and perched there, head cocked and cheeping like he owned the place. If only I could get outside, I'd show him a thing or two.

Suddenly he took off in a flurry of wings. I leaned forward to see what had scared him, and a cat hopped onto the bench—a black cat with trim white-mitten paws.

Alice!

I jumped up and pressed my nose against the glass. *Look this way, Alice!*

She was still staring at the bird, which had flitted back to the bush.

Look over here! I meowed and rubbed against the glass.

Robin walked by again. "What *is* the matter, Briggston?" she asked. "Why are you so intent on going outside?" She looked out the door. "Oh, that's it! There's a lady cat out there you'd like to meet." She bent down and gave me a pat. "Sorry, old boy. One cat is enough for me —especially with you acting so strangely lately."

She left, but my eyes stayed fastened on Alice. I pressed my face to the glass again, and this time she spotted me! Her ears shot straight up, and then her tail did, too. She hopped off the bench and bounded to the door.

"George!" she said. Or at least that's what I think she said. I couldn't actually hear her voice through the glass.

Her mouth moved again. I tilted my head and swiveled my ears, hoping she'd realize I couldn't hear what she was saying. If only I could get outside, Alice would lead me to Twila, and Twila would take me home!

I heard footsteps behind me, then Robin was bending down to scratch my ears. She had a huge purple bag slung over her shoulder and a jacket folded over her arm. "Time for me to go home, Briggston. It's up to you to hold down the fort."

I looked around quickly, wondering if "fort" was a different word for "grasshopper" and if I would be allowed to eat it instead of just holding it down. As Robin reached for the door, I gathered my feet beneath me, ready to make a dash toward freedom, all the while trying to look nonchalant, as if escaping was the last thing on my mind.

Robin wasn't fooled. She kept her eyes on me as she opened the door a crack. "You stay right there, Briggston. I don't need you roaming the neighborhood with a stray cat." She glanced outside and I did, too. Alice was no longer standing by the door. "I see your friend has left."

That's what she thought. *I* could still see Alice. She was crouched between the bench and the brick wall of the library, tail flicking.

"Briggs, you can't go outside. You don't like it out there anyway, you crazy cat. I don't know what's gotten into you." She wasn't taking her eyes off of me.

Which meant she wasn't watching for Alice. I waved my tail like a signal flag, hoping that Alice would understand what I wanted her to do.

"No, Briggston. You stay in here." Robin opened the door a little wider.

I crept forward. Just a little. Close enough to keep her focused on me, but not close enough that she could brush me out of the way.

Her mouth set into a line. I've seen the same look on Emma's face just before she shuts me out of the barn so I can't get to the pan of milk she's poured for my Aunt

Eloise. As if I'd really drink Aunt Eloise's milk. Well, at least not all of it.

"Good night, Briggston." Robin slipped out of the door, shutting it quickly behind her. She didn't notice, though, that Alice had crept inside and was now tucked into a bottom bookshelf not far from the door, safely out of sight.

8

PLENTY OF PROBLEMS

I scrambled to the door and plastered my face against the glass, watching Robin until she'd driven away. Then I let out my breath. "Okay. It's safe now," I said, turning to Alice.

She bounded over and gave my ears a lick. "You're a sight for sore eyes, George. I was worried I'd never see you again!"

"That makes two of us. Robin, the lady here at the library, picked me up at The Vet's. She thinks I'm her cat named—"

"Briggston," Alice finished for me.

"How'd you know that?"

"Briggston's at the farm," she said. "Lil brought him home thinking he was you."

"Lil?" My whiskers bristled. "Why her? Why not Emma?"

"Emma was busy and asked Lil if she'd run some errands. Lil knows The Vet pretty well since Felix's visit there."

Well, that made sense. Lil *had* spent a lot of time at The Vet after Felix was nearly eaten by Old Mangy earlier this summer. Old Mangy had been sending too many of us farm animals to The Vet lately.

I twitched my tail in irritation. "I would've thought that even Lil could tell the difference between that lazy lump of a cat and me."

"Well, the two of you do look amazingly alike." Alice sat and wrapped her tail around her white-mitten paws.

I laid back my ears. "*You* weren't fooled."

Alice head-butted my shoulder. "Of course not. Felix and I knew there was a problem the minute Briggston arrived at the farm. He streaked into Lil's house as soon as she opened the pet carrier, hid behind the couch, and refused to come out."

Now my ears shot straight up. "And Lil let him stay? Lil *never* lets *me* into her house." Not since I'd supposedly shredded one of her best blankets. I'd only loosened a few threads, but she claimed I'd ruined it.

"Briggston was obviously terrified, and Lil felt sorry for him. Or rather, sorry for him thinking he was you. She let him stay until he settled down, then he purred and rubbed her legs and acted so well-mannered that she let him stay overnight, and now…" Alice shook her head. "Now she's decided she must've misjudged you because you're—or rather, he's—so calm and polite. She's letting Briggston stay inside as long as he likes."

Calm and polite? Briggston was definitely pulling the wool over her eyes. "And Felix is letting this happen? He wasn't so happy when *I* was in his house."

"He's too busy trying to keep the farm under control to be sitting around on the porch," Alice said. "There's a family of gophers who've moved into the garden from the meadow, and a weasel who has his eye on the chickens thinking that Emma might forget to lock them in their house some night. And Old Mangy's still roaming around, too."

"Old Mangy? He didn't vamoose?"

Alice rolled her eyes. "No. He's taken you up on your offer and has been coming over every night to finish what's left in the dog bowls. The dogs are so terrified of him that they've hardly been eating anything lately, thinking that if they don't leave him enough, he'll go after them."

"Why don't they just chase him off? They did a good enough job chasing me around the farm when Felix ordered them to."

"Mangy has bigger teeth than you do. And he smells a lot worse, too." Her nose twitched.

"Well, the smell should be an advantage. Dogs seem to like smelly things. The smellier the better."

Alice rubbed her nose. "Not in this case. Whenever

they get a whiff of that coyote, they get out of the way. Felix has been trying to get the dogs to help him, but they're a little…" Her eyes narrowed like she was trying to think of a polite way to say what she was thinking.

"They're distractible," I said. "And not just a little. They're a *lot* distractible."

Alice nodded. "That's probably the best way to put it. Felix sends them out to the garden to patrol for gophers, and they end up swimming in the pond or chasing birds through the meadow instead."

"What about Kid?" Kid might only be a half-grown Muscovy duck, but she had enough gumption and guts to patrol the farm by herself if she had to.

Alice shook her head. "Emma's locked Kid in the chicken pen again, supposedly to keep her safe until you've returned to your duties."

I rubbed a paw over my ears. "I'll bet Kid's not very happy about that."

Alice's whiskers twitched. "No, not at all. She keeps trying to escape, but Emma's too quick."

"I can sympathize." I flicked the end of my tail. "What's Emma doing about all of this? Surely she suspects something is wrong if that lazy lump of a cat refuses to come outside."

"She's busy cleaning out the garden and hasn't been paying much attention. She told Lil that if you wanted to stay in her house until your leg healed, you could."

My fur poofed. The farm *was* falling apart, and my

human couldn't even tell the difference between me and an imposter. Alice started licking my fur back into place, but I didn't let her distract me. "Tomorrow morning you have to help me break out of this place," I said. "We'll get Twila to take me home."

Alice stopped licking. "Uh, George. Twila's house is clear across town." She patted my stick leg with her paw. "I don't think you'd make it. Besides—"

I could feel my fur bristling. "You think I'm too weak?"

"George, don't be ridiculous. You're not weak, you're hurt. You need to heal and then you can—"

I sneezed, loudly enough to show my annoyance. "There's no time for that. If you think I'm too weak to walk across town, then you need to find a way to get Twila to come *here*."

"George, that's what I was getting ready to say. Twila was already here today. Didn't you see her?"

I blinked, trying to figure out how I could have missed her. "No. Maybe she was here while I was napping."

"Well, she saw you. She came home and commented on how much the library cat looks like George. She's said that before, but I'd never paid much attention until today. I got to wondering if the library cat could be you—or rather, if Briggston could be the library cat and that you'd been mistaken for him. That's why I walked all the way across town to come and see." She scanned the room. "I've never been to the library before."

I glanced at the shelves. "I don't know why humans

think this is such an interesting place. The stacks around here are made of books instead of hay and they aren't for climbing. Robin has made that very clear. And good luck finding a grasshopper or mouse to chase." I sank my claws into the rug. "I'm going to go crazy if I'm trapped inside much longer."

"Poor George." Alice started licking my shoulder, probably thinking she needed to provide some calming therapy.

But I didn't have time to relax. I needed to get home! I leaned out of range of her tongue. "If Twila's already found me, why hasn't she brought Emma to rescue me?"

Alice shook her head. "You don't understand. She said you *looked* like George. She didn't say you *were* George. She thinks George is back on the farm. *All* of the humans think you're on the farm. That's why this is such a problem."

I dug my claws further into the rug and pulled until I could feel a few threads popping loose. "If I could just get out the door! But this stupid leg slows me down too much."

We sat in silence a moment. Well, silence except for the sound of my claws shredding the rug. I didn't know what Alice was pondering, but I was trying to figure out a plan for escape.

Suddenly Alice pricked up her ears. "I hear a mouse!" she whispered, and started slinking toward the story time corner.

I pricked up my ears, too, but all I could hear were the

guinea pigs rustling in their cage. I shook my head. "Alice —wait."

She turned and frowned at me. "*Shh*. You'll give us away."

I stood and limped toward the corner, giving her shoulder a swipe with my tongue as I passed. "You've got to see this," I said as I led the way to the rodent cage.

9

OF RODENTS AND READING

"These," I said, when we'd reached the tall cage, "are guinea pigs."

Posha and Pearl were at their food dish, jaws grinding. When they saw us, they stopped chewing.

Pearl pointed her nose in Alice's direction. "Who are you?"

Alice flicked the tip of her tail back and forth, like she was unsure whether to introduce herself or pounce. I knew just how she felt.

"These are the *library* guinea pigs," I said, nudging her shoulder. Then I turned to the rodents. "This is my friend, Alice."

"Is she going to live here, too?"

"No, she just came to rescue me."

The rodents looked at each other. "*Rescue At Sea!*"

Posha squeaked, and clambered on top of their plastic hut with her nose poked into the air as if she were gasping for her last breath. "The ship is going down. Waves are crashing over the bow."

I stared at her. "What?"

"The book *Rescue At Sea*," she replied. "One of the kids read part of it to me last week. Great plot. Not enough pictures."

"Oka-a-a-a-y," I said.

"We've read about rescues from avalanches, rescues from floods, rescues from caves. Rescues are my favorite. Lots of action." Posha scrambled down from the hut and poked her nose through the wire. "Are you in danger? Are you mortally wounded?"

"What?"

Pearl started scrabbling through the wood shavings at the bottom of her cage. "We could make a bandage with some of our newspaper or send up smoke signals for help!"

Now both rodents were digging through their litter so energetically that shavings spewed out of the cage in a fine cloud. I sneezed.

Alice was snorting, too, but it sounded more like a laugh than a dust problem.

"These gals are crazy," I said, nudging her. "Now that you know they're not mice, let's get out of here."

"Wait." Alice didn't budge. "I want to know what they're talking about."

Pearl stopped digging and looked up. "What do you mean?"

Posha stopped scrabbling, too. "Maybe they haven't read the same books we have, Pearly." She poked her nose in the direction of the shelves across the corner from us. "Maybe they only read from the nonfiction section."

The rodents looked at each other. "If only we could get to the nonfiction section," said Pearl, as if she were wishing for a heaping pile of guinea pig treats. Then she turned to me. "Can you really open our cage door, or were you just joking?"

I glanced at the wire door. It didn't have a slidey bolt latch like the gate on the chicken pen. When Robin had opened it this morning to fill the food bowl, it looked like she'd just pulled the door straight down. But I hadn't really been paying attention. "Probably, if I watched Robin do it a couple more times." I tilted my head. "Why do you want to get out so badly? Aren't you afraid I might have you for a snack?"

Posha snorted. "Why would you eat us when Robin stuffs you with all you can hold?"

I opened my mouth to tell her that I never turn down a snack, then closed it. She was right. With all of the kibbles and kitty treats Robin had given me today, I wasn't feeling very hungry.

Then Pearl scrambled up to the top of their hut, striking a pose as if surveying the room. "We're explorers!" she squeaked. "Sailing the great seas in search of whales, trekking through the jungles looking for monkeys, climbing mountains to find mountain goats."

"What?" I swiveled my ears to make sure I'd heard correctly. "Whales, monkeys, mountain goats…what are those?"

"Dunno," said Posha. "But we'd like to find out, and we can't if we're stuck in this cage."

"Uh, I hate to tell you this, but there are no mountain goats in this place. No regular goats, either." And I *did* know what *they* were.

"Might be in those books over there, though." Pearl pointed her nose to the shelves across from their cage.

I'd met some crazy animals in my day, but these gals were definitely the craziest. "A book would be a terrible hiding place for an animal," I said. "There's not room inside for anything bigger than a flea." Unless it was one of those flattened animals I'd seen at story time, but I didn't really want to think about that. "You probably just want something to chew on." In my experience, that's what rodents did best. The mice in Emma's barn chewed wood, cardboard boxes, labels on cans, whatever was left lying around.

Posha rolled her round, black eyes. "No, silly. Books aren't hiding places, and they're not for chewing, either— well, not right away, at least. You *read* them first."

Alice pricked up her ears. "You can read?"

Posha and Pearl looked at each other, then back at her. "Can't you?"

"No." Alice leaned closer to the cage. "I thought that was something only humans did."

"Wait a minute," I said. "What's this reading thing?"

"It's..." Alice paused. "I'm not sure what it is. I just know that every evening Twila sits on the couch and opens a book and stares at it. She calls it 'reading.'"

"What's she looking at?" I asked, trying to picture Twila sitting and staring at a book. She hadn't done that when I was living in her house as a kitten. But then again, we kittens had never been allowed to wander the house. We'd stayed in the kitchen or on the porch.

Before she could answer, Pearl put her nose in the air. "All guinea pigs are taught to read," she said. "Posha and I cut our teeth on *The Times*. Our mother always insisted on the very best."

"Oka-a-a-a-y," I said. I had no idea what the little looney was talking about.

Posha must've noticed my blank expression. She began digging under the wood shavings at the bottom of the cage again. It didn't take her long to uncover some paper and pull it to the surface.

"Newspaper!" she squeaked. "All humans use the stuff to line the bottoms of cages. It's covered with these squiggly lines called letters, and the letters go together to make words, see? So if we want to find out what's going on in town, we read the words on the front page. If we'd rather have a laugh, we read the comics. If we're feeling bored…" she said, nose twitching, "…then we chew on it. Nothing like digesting some good information."

They both chittered loudly.

"Oka-a-a-a-y," I said again. My head was spinning with all this new information. I still didn't understand how squiggly lines could be words since words are something you *say* and squiggles are something you *see*, but I didn't have time to listen to any more rodent ramblings on the subject. I needed to be planning with Alice how to get home.

"Alice—" I started.

"Hold on, George," she said. "I'm interested in this reading thing. Let's find out how they do it." She leaned closer to the guinea pigs. "So what's going on in town?"

The rodents looked at each other. Posha began doing little jumpy skips in the wood dust like a miniature bucking horse. Pearl leaped down from the hut and did a twirl. "Do we have something to show you!" she squeaked, disappearing inside their purple plastic hut.

10

A FAIR DEAL

It didn't take long before Pearl emerged from the hut carrying a partially shredded piece of newspaper in her mouth. She flattened it against the wire for me to see. I wasn't impressed. So much excitement for that? It was just a ratty piece of paper covered with those squiggly black lines Posha had called letters.

I moved a little closer to the cage, thinking I'd try the staring technique Alice had mentioned. But even after looking at the letters until my eyes crossed, they still looked like a bunch of meaningless squiggles.

"See?" Posha said, obviously assuming I'd been staring at the paper hard enough to make sense of it all. "It says that the county fair will be held in one week at the local fairgrounds. That's what Robin talked about at story time today. There will be a pie baking contest, a barbecue contest, a hot dog eating contest…"

My eyes went wide. If I were home, I'd definitely be warning Festus and Brutus, the two bowsers there, to stay away from the fair. If humans were having a dog eating contest, they didn't want to be caught in the action. I was just relieved it wasn't a hot *cat* eating contest.

I definitely needed to get back to the more important task at hand—planning my escape with Alice—but before I could get Alice's attention, Pearl dropped the paper and started whirling around the cage, whistling. "That's the good part, that's the good part."

"What? Eating hot dogs?" I couldn't imagine a guinea pig trying to eat a dog.

Posha looked at me like my nose had turned purple. "No, silly. Weren't you listening? The pet dress-up contest!" She covered one eye with her paw. "I'd make a great pirate."

Pearl shook her head. "The judges go for cute, Posh. My vote's for being cheerleaders."

"Wait a minute!" Alice sprang to her feet. "You're going to the pet show at the fair?"

"Yup, we always do," Posha said, scratching an ear with her back paw. "The kids choose costumes for us, and we always win first place."

"George, I've got a great idea," Alice said. "Felix and I will convince Lil to take you—that is, Briggston—to the fair, and you get Robin to take you. Then you two can switch places while you're there."

"Oooh," the rodents said in unison.

Posha ran up the ramp to the second level and looked me over. "I've got it!" she squeaked. "Pearl and I are the pirates, and you can be the evil sea monster. The kids can bring a costume for you, too!"

I backed away. "No way am I getting into a costume. The last time that happened, I became the community laughing stock. Never again."

"But George—" Alice began.

"But nothing." I turned and started to stalk away.

I was stopped by a shrill squeak from behind me. "Hold on, cat. Maybe we can work out a deal."

My fur poofed slightly. The last animal I'd made a deal with had been Old Mangy. If he didn't eat me, then he went free. That deal didn't seem to be working out too well.

"Not interested," I said. "If it has anything to do with dressing up, it's not going to happen."

"George, quit being so stubborn. At least listen," Alice said.

I huffed. "Fine. I'll listen to their deal, then you and I need to go somewhere quiet and come up with a real plan."

Pearl and Posha had their noses together, rumbling and whispering about something. Posha looked at me. "I think we can work something out for you," she said. "Did you see that big purple bag Robin carries with her when she leaves?"

I twitched my tail, wanting to end this conversation and get back to the important stuff. "Yeah. So?"

"She carries it with her wherever she goes," Pearl said. "Even when she takes us to the fair. She always has books in it, and other stuff, too—like our costumes."

I glanced at Alice and she tilted her head, looking just as confused as I. "And this is important because…?" I said.

Posha rumbled. "The bag is big enough to hold a cat. I'm sure it is. Briggston crawls inside it sometimes."

Ah! Suddenly the bag's significance became clear. "If I got into the bag, then I could sneak to the fair without having to dress up."

"Exactly!" Pearl was dashing from one end of the cage to the other. "But only if Robin doesn't notice. And that's where we come in. She'll set the bag down on the ground when she puts us in our pet carrier. If we distract her, you'll have time to crawl inside and bury yourself under our costumes."

That might actually work. I twisted my whiskers with a paw. "You said this was a deal. What do you want from me?"

"Freedom!" Both guinea pigs squeaked so loudly that my whiskers practically frazzled. "You figure out a way to open the cage and let us out every night between now and the day of the fair."

"Yeah, right," I said. "And you'll have so much fun

scurrying around and chewing books that you won't want to go back into your cage, and when Robin comes back in the morning, she'll lay the blame for all the destruction and mayhem on me. Then she'll lock me in her office every night. I know how that works."

"We won't! We won't!" the guinea pigs squealed.

"We'll go back inside the cage when we need to," said Posha.

"And we promise not to nibble a single book," said Pearl. "At least, not enough that Robin will notice."

I frowned and looked at Alice. She was a pretty good judge of character. "What do you think? Should I believe them?"

Her whiskers twitched. I didn't know if she was trying not to laugh at the pigs, or trying not to laugh at me. "I think it's a wonderful idea. Especially since you're being stubborn about not wearing a costume."

I rolled my eyes. "Super. Great. The deal's on. I'll watch Robin open the cage tomorrow and work on letting you loose tomorrow night. Just so you know, though, any bad behavior on your part might make me grumpy. And when I get grumpy, I get hungry."

The rodents chittered to each other and started doing little hops into the air. "Freedom, freedom, freedom!"

"Let's get out of here," I said to Alice, having to raise my voice to be heard over the tumult. "We need to make our own plans."

We spent the rest of the night discussing the best way

to convince Lil to take Briggston to the fair. I decided to leave that one in Felix's hands. Lil was his human, and I'd learned from experience that Lil acted a *lot* differently than Emma.

When Robin returned the next morning, I made sure I was close to the glass door, but not too close. Since Robin had her eyes on me, she didn't notice as Alice slipped off the bottom shelf nearby and through the crack in the closing door.

Alice had the hardest part of the plan to put into action. She had to convince Twila to take her to the farm. Then she had to help Felix and the other animals figure out how to get Briggston dressed up and to the fair.

My part of the operation was fairly simple in comparison. All I needed to do was to figure out how to open the rodents' cage and make sure they stayed out of trouble. Easy-peasy, right?

Ha!

11

STICK LEGS ALL AROUND

After I watched Alice disappear down the street, I went over to where Robin was standing behind the circulation desk, hoping maybe she'd have more kitty treats. I rubbed against her legs to get her attention, and she bent down and held out her hand. "Good morning, Briggs. Sleep well?"

She wasn't offering any kitty treats, but I let her rub my ears just so she'd feel useful. Then I watched carefully as she reached into her big purple bag. I got a little excited when she pulled out a plastic sack that smelled vaguely familiar. Then I realized it was stuffed full with carrot chunks and peels. I know all about carrots because Emma grows them in her garden. Humans seem to like them. But not me.

I wrinkled my nose and considered going back to my basket for a nap. It'd been a long night after all. But Robin didn't seem interested in snacking on the carrots herself. Instead, she walked to the guinea pigs' cage, rattling the bag and saying "treat, treat," all the way. The rodents started squeaking and squealing so loudly I wanted to cover my ears and run in the other direction.

Duty is duty, however. If Robin was going to open the cage door, I needed to observe more closely. I clumped after her. When she reached the cage, she took hold of the door and gave it a tug. It came down in her hand like a ramp, making a nice wide path for escape. But the rodents weren't thinking about that. They were too busy running in circles and kicking up sawdust.

Robin dumped the carrot treats into their bowl and the rodents immediately starting devouring them. I suddenly understood why they were called pigs. No table manners at all. Pearl had both paws in the bowl, probably trying to cover the food so Posha couldn't reach it. Posha wasn't paying any attention to her, though. She was too busy gobbling the stray carrot peels that had landed outside the bowl.

Robin laughed. "Enjoy your breakfast, you two." She closed the cage door by lifting it back into place and giving it a good thrust forward. There was a click as it latched.

I stuck around after she left, fascinated by the rodents' performance. They were gobbling the carrot peels so quickly, it reminded me of the time I'd seen Emma's nephew suck spaghetti into his mouth, strand by strand. I'd been watching him eat his lunch on the porch that day, ready to clean up any mess the kid might make. He hadn't dropped any of his spaghetti then, and these rodents weren't dropping their carrot peels now. Not that I would've been interested in cleaning up *their* mess.

Posha finally noticed me. She gulped down the last of her peel. "Did you see how she opened the door?"

Pearl stopped chewing and looked at me, too, with part of a peel still hanging from her mouth.

I nodded. "All she did was pull it down."

"So you can get us out tonight?" Posha grabbed another peel and began chewing again.

I hesitated. If the cage was so easy to open, why couldn't the rodents just lean on the door and open it themselves?

"Remember, you help us and we'll help you." Pearl chomped down the last of her peel.

"Sure. I'll get you out tonight. No problem." With that, I went back to my basket. I needed some sleep, especially if I had to supervise the rodents this evening. I laid back my ears just thinking about it. Rodents running into tiny corners, rodents chewing on books, rodents refusing to return to their cage. Yes, I definitely needed some sleep. Tonight promised to be long and exhausting.

* * *

I was awakened by a high voice speaking very close to my ear. "Briggston, it's story time. You want to hear a story?"

I opened an eye. A little boy was crouching beside my basket. When he saw me looking at him, he picked me up and lugged me over to the story corner where lots of other kids were sitting on pillows, chattering.

Robin was perched on a chair in front of the group. She smiled when she saw me coming. "You found a friend, Briggston."

I didn't recall looking for one. I figured I could get rid of the unwanted attention by doing a little scratching and clawing. On the other paw, I was becoming curious about this reading thing. If the guinea pigs could figure it out, surely I could too. And listening to Posha and Pearl talk, I realized there were plenty of critters I knew nothing about. Being a good security chief, I wanted to learn as much as possible in case something strange showed up on our farm. Emma had brought home a goat once. For all I knew, she might show up with one of those mountain goats the rodents had mentioned.

So I let the kid pull me onto his lap.

Robin opened a book and turned it toward us. I stared. Inside the book was a *really* strange, flattened human. He had a stick leg just like me, and a patch covering one eye. It looked like he'd been in a fight with a coyote, too, and had ended up worse off than me.

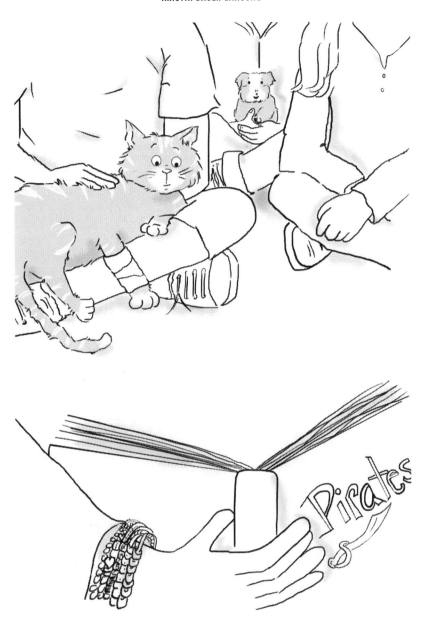

I was trying to figure out how a human could be flattened and pressed into a book when Robin started talking and turning the pages. I leaned closer. The stick-leg man was surrounded by other strange humans. *All* of them looked like they'd been in a coyote fight. Some had stick legs and eye patches, and some had hooks instead of hands. But there wasn't a coyote in sight.

It wouldn't have been easy for a coyote to get to them, anyway. The humans were standing on some sort of house thing, but the house was surrounded by water. On one page, a human was even walking down a wooden plank and jumping into the water.

I shuddered. No cat in his right mind would jump into water.

When Robin finally shut the book, the kids started chattering again. One of them stood up and pulled some tiny clothes out of a bag. "For Posha and Pearl," he announced.

It wasn't until then that I noticed the guinea pigs. They were also listening to the story, sitting in the laps of a couple of the kids. A flurry of activity ensued as several kids helped dress the pigs in the costumes. Finally the rodents were placed on Robin's lap for everyone to see. They looked distinctly like the strange humans from the book: Posha had an eye patch and Pearl had a little stick leg.

One of the kids turned and looked at me. "We should dress Briggston up like a pirate, too!"

My fur poofed. I already had a stick leg. If they gave me another, I wouldn't be able to walk! I struggled out of the arms that'd been holding me and galumphed toward Robin's office, hoping to find someplace to hide.

A couple kids started after me, but Robin said, "Let him go. If Briggston doesn't want a costume, that's okay."

Whew! I didn't take any chances, though. I decided to finish my nap curled up on the floor in a corner of the office instead of returning to my—that is, Briggston's—basket behind the circulation desk.

Later, Robin woke me when she came into the office. She stuffed several books into her big bag, then walked over to me. "Okay, Briggs. Time for you to get back to your own bed. I don't want you in here overnight."

Me neither. I trooped down the hallway and watched Robin head for the door. If I could sneak out, I wouldn't have to worry about opening a cage door for the rodents or hitching a ride to a place where humans ate dogs. But Robin was one sharp human. She didn't open the glass door until she knew exactly where I was. Then she watched me like a hawk while she slipped out.

So once again I was locked in the library for the night, but without Alice for company this time—just a couple wise-cracking rodents whom I couldn't even eat. It was enough to make me want to shred something. My claws hooked into the mat by the door, but they weren't able to gain much traction on the short, stubbly surface. And the rubber coating on the bottom repelled my claws, too. Not satisfying at all.

My whiskers drooped. This was looking to be a long, long night, and there wasn't a thing I could do about it.

12

JAIL BREAK

No use sitting around moping about my problems. I didn't have a good companion for the evening, but I did have a job—and duty was duty. I stiffened my whiskers and stalked over to the guinea pigs' cage. Might as well get the night's activities underway. Peering through the wire, I could see two furry lumps tucked away inside the plastic hut. Probably both fast asleep. That was okay by me. I could try opening the door without them staring at me.

I balanced on my stick leg and wrapped my good paw around the wire, like I'd seen Robin do with her fingers. Then I gave a tug. Nothing happened. Another tug, just a little harder. I could feel the door wiggle and shift slightly. Good grief. How hard was I going to have to pull?

The rodents poked their noses out of the hut. "Hey!" said Pearl. "Are you letting us out?"

"I'm trying," I said. "The door isn't as easy to open as I thought."

"We can help," Posha squeaked. And before I could say anything, both pigs had scurried over and plunked their front feet against the wire, all set to push from their side.

Well, no harm in trying. I gave another tug, and another. Each time, the door jiggled a little more. The guinea pigs weren't adding much muscle, but they were heavy enough to tilt the door in the right direction.

I gave one more gigantic heave, and the door slammed open right on top of my head. I hissed and sprang backward, which caused the door to bang against the floor. The guinea pigs sprawled across the opening, paddling their forefeet between the wires until they finally gained traction and clambered onto the floor.

"Freedom!" squeaked Posha, kicking up her heels. She scooted toward the far bookshelf with Pearl close behind.

Instantly I went into a crouch, tail flicking. Couldn't help it. The rodents looked too much like a meal. I squeezed my eyes closed and forced myself to sit down. If I hadn't needed to guard the books, I would've just walked away.

Something rustled above me and I looked up to see Bobby Scales, head erect, watching the rodents. Good thing he was tucked away in his glass box or he'd probably be wanting to chase them, too.

"Freedom," the reptile hissed, his tongue flicking in and out of his mouth.

"No can do, buddy," I said. "I don't want you out and about chasing the guinea pigs. Then I *would* get into trouble."

The snake looked down at me. "Why would I chasssse the pigssss?"

I frowned. "That's what snakes do. Well, they chase mice more than guinea pigs, I suppose. But a rodent is a rodent."

"But why would a ssssnake want to chasssse a mousssse?"

My whiskers twitched. This was one clueless reptile. "To eat them, of course." Then I started to wonder. "What does Robin feed you? Kibbles?" It wouldn't surprise me.

Bobby Scales' head swayed back and forth. "Robin givesss me a mousssse every week, but it'ssss ssssstiff and doessssn't move."

"Ah, already dead then." I wondered if Briggston caught the mice and then Robin put them in the cage for Bobby. I scratched my ear. No, that lazy lump of a cat didn't appear to be smart enough to catch anything faster than a few Zs. "Too bad, buddy. You're missing out on the thrill of the chase."

"Thrill?" Bobby was watching the guinea pigs again. The rodents had managed to scale the pile of pillows to reach one of the top shelves and had tipped over a book that'd been sitting there. They were staring at one of the pages, squeaking to each other.

"Thrill," I repeated. "A good chase really gets the blood pumping. And then to eat something you've caught all by yourself—it doesn't get much better than that."

"Hmmm." Bobby looked down at me. "I'm not ssssure I believe you."

I stood. "Probably just as well you don't, stuck in that box like you are. You don't have a choice." I almost felt sorry for the guy. What a life. Trapped in a glass cage and fed dead mice. "Happy napping."

I padded over to a nearby pillow. Might as well get comfortable if I was going to watch these rodents all night.

13

LESSONS ON LIONS (AND SNAKES)

The rodents were good to their word and didn't nibble on any books, although it was a little tricky getting them back into their cage before Robin arrived the next morning. They were absolutely head over heels with excitement about the books and wanted to look through every one. We had a few tense moments when they threatened to back out on our deal, wanting to keep me here at the library until they'd read all the books on all the shelves.

A terrible image had flashed through my head: me, stuck in this sterile building until I was too old to hobble after the guinea pigs, let alone chase mice back at the farm. Luckily I was able to convince the rodent pair that since they'd helped me open their cage door, they could easily train Briggston to open it, too.

I didn't tell the rodents that, based on my brief introduction to Briggston at The Vet's, I was concerned he'd be too uncooperative to be helpful. But Briggston would have to be the rodents' problem. *My* problem was getting back home before the mice took over the farm.

I spent the rest of the morning curled in my basket, exhausted from watching guinea pigs all night. Good thing none of the farm animals were here to see me babysitting rodents. I'd be the target for bad jokes the rest of my life.

Another kid pulled me out of my basket for story time that afternoon. I tried to let him know that I was needing my sleep, but he ignored my puffed fur and twitching tail. Robin frowned at me from where she was standing behind the circulation desk. My attendance was evidently required, so I let myself be dragged along.

The kids at story time had brought another set of guinea pig costumes—cheerleaders this time. Celia found a book about cheerleaders and turned the pages so everyone could see the strange, flat humans inside doing flips and jumps and standing on top of each other. I tried to picture Posha or Pearl flipping in the air, but failed. Pearl was super excited the rest of the day, though, and tried out some skips and flips that evening while she was scrambling through the book shelves.

The next day the kids brought cowboy and lion costumes to story time. I'd heard of cowboys from my human, Ted. I didn't know anything about lions, though. The lion costumes made me think a lion might be a really hairy miniature cow with a super long tail. When I asked the guinea pigs if I was right, they whistled and squeaked until my ears were fit to burst.

That night Posha said she was going to show me what a real lion looked like. She scurried through the shelves until she found a book she called an encyclopedia of animals. I figured that meant it was a book about animals on bicycles. Nope. No bicycles. But the book did have lots of flat animals. I was truly grateful that Emma didn't do that to any of *her* animals.

Pearl was turning pages in the encyclopedia when Bobby Scales hissed that he wanted to see, too. I did feel kind of sorry for him, trapped in that glass box. So I used my head to nudge the book across the floor until it was right below his shelf where he could see it. He and I both watched while Pearl found the page about lions.

Lions turned out to be very strange-looking cats. The one in the book had wild hair all around his head. He looked like he needed to be sheared like Emma's sheep. But the guinea pigs read that lions were very big and dangerous and weren't kept on farms. The lion in the book didn't look too big to me, but maybe it'd been shrunk along with being flattened.

Then the guinea pigs flipped through the pages and told me about some of the other flattened animals. There was an animal called an elephant who had the longest nose I'd ever seen. I wouldn't want to be near one of those guys if he had to sneeze! Some fancy-looking birds called peacocks had tails so long that I figured they'd be easy-peasy to catch. Too bad we didn't have any critters like that on our farm.

"Are there sssnakesss in that book?" asked Bobby.

"Sure thing," said Posha. She and Pearl pushed through plenty of pages until they were almost to the back of the book. The "ess" section, they called it, which was a word I'd never heard before. I didn't know what esses had to do with snakes, but the guinea pigs found several pages of snakes right where they said they would.

I recognized bull snakes and garter snakes right off, since there are several who live in the pasture and meadow on our farm. I'd never seen most of the other kinds of snakes, though. Some were hanging from trees. Others were crawling through sand. One was squeezing a bird in its coils, and one had its jaws open wide enough to swallow the mouse sitting right beside it. Stupid rodent. Should've run while it had the chance.

Posha took a look at the snake who was about to swallow the mouse and gave a squeak. "That's horrible!"

She started to turn the page, but Bobby said, "Wait!" He plastered his face against the glass and stared down at the book. "What doessss it ssssay?"

Posha and Pearl looked at each other, kind of like they couldn't decide whether to slam the book closed or skedaddle or maybe both.

Before they could make up their minds, Bobby asked, "What'sss wrong? Can't you read thossse wordsss?"

The snake was definitely smarter than I thought. Posha

rumbled a bit and puffed herself up. "I can read *anything*," she said.

"Sssso prove it," Bobby said. "Read that page to me."

Posha and Pearl chittered to each other, then Posha cleared her throat and looked down at the book. "'Snakes are carnivores, which means they eat meat instead of plants. But they don't use their teeth to chew their food like you and I do. Their teeth are used for grabbing and holding their prey. A snake will open its mouth wide and swallow its meal whole, in one gulp. Small snakes eat small things like insects or bird eggs. Bigger snakes eat birds, fish, frogs, and rodents, such as prairie dogs and…uh… other things…and…uh…' That's enough of that."

She and Pearl quickly slammed the book closed and scuttled away to find a different one.

"Sssseemssss you were right," said Bobby.

"Told you so," I said. Not that I was trying to brag or anything, but Bobby Scales was a snake and he had the right to know how a snake was supposed to behave.

I pushed the book back to the shelf where we'd found it. Robin would put it away for us in the morning. She'd grumble a little, like she did every morning, and would scold me about making a mess. But she hadn't threatened to lock me in the office yet.

The rodents were busy examining a pile of books that I'd already knocked down for them. Several were about pirates, one was about cheerleaders, and two had flattened cowboys inside. I could hear the guinea pigs arguing about which book to read first, and I decided I didn't want to stick around and find out who won. If they'd been talking more about lions—well, then I might've stayed.

I padded back to my basket and had just settled into a wonderful dream about chasing guinea pigs through stacks of books when the sharp whistles from my dream guinea pigs became so loud they woke me up. That's when I realized Posha and Pearl were squeaking for real—and they sounded terrified.

14

SNAKE ATTACK!

I hobbled to the story corner as fast as my stick leg would take me, just in time to see Bobby Scales slithering across the floor hot on Posha's tail—or round backside, as the case may be. The rodent was squealing for dear life, scrambling from book stack to book stack, trying to keep something between herself and the crazed snake. Pearl was also shrieking from where she was huddled on one of the bottom bookshelves, probably hoping she was hidden. Crazy rodent.

I glanced quickly up to Bobby's glass box and saw that one corner of the cover had been pushed aside. I hadn't realized the snake could get out or I wouldn't have been filling his head with tales of rodent hunting.

"Get back to your cage!" I shouted to Pearl.

Bobby had managed to trap Posha and was opening

his jaws wider…and wider…and wider. Good thing Posha was so well rounded. It gave me time to blunder across the room, pounce on the reptile's back, and dig in my one good set of front claws.

That got Bobby's attention. He swiveled around and turned his jaws on me. I blundered backward before realizing that I was much too big to fit inside his mouth. So I pounced again, trying to avoid his teeth and hold onto his writhing body at the same time. I felt a little like one of those cowboys from the books, trying to ride a bucking bronco.

"Get back to the cage!" I shouted again, this time to Posha who seemed frozen in place. She shook herself out of her stupor and raced back to the cage as fast as a plump rodent with short legs can run. Pearl had outpaced her and was already inside the cage, huddled in the hut.

When Posha was nearly to the cage, I jumped off the snake and stumbled after her. I could hear Bobby slithering behind me, catching up. I tried to hobble faster, but the snake reached out and tangled himself around one of my back legs.

I fell forward onto my nose. Ouch!

Then Bobby slid past me, heading straight for the open doorway of the guinea pigs' cage. If he got inside, it would be a disaster. He'd have them trapped inside their little hut!

I pushed myself onto my feet, caught hold of Bobby's tail, and ran up the length of his back, leaving claw marks the entire way. That slowed him down long enough for me to get to the cage door first. I skidded to a stop and whirled around, glaring at the approaching reptile.

"What do you think you're doing?" I growled, blocking the open doorway with my body.

"Only what you ssssaid I should," Bobby replied. He reared up, probably looking for a way to get around me.

"I said snakes hunt rodents. I didn't say *you* should hunt them."

Bobby wavered. "But I'm a ssssnake."

"Who has a human to feed you."

Bobby lowered his head slightly, like Brutus or Festus when they're being scolded. "What'ssss the fun in that? I alwayssss felt like I was missssing out on ssssomething and now I know what that issss." He dipped his head even further. "I thought you would undersssstand."

I carefully maneuvered so I could snag the wire door with the claws of my good front leg and push it closed, all the while keeping a wary eye on Bobby. "I'm sorry to discourage you, friend," I said, "but this is not the time or place for you to develop a predator's instinct. Not if you want to stay on your human's good side."

Bobby's head sank all the way to the ground. "Sssso when issss a good time?"

The wire door thudded against the cage. One more bump from my hind end and it clicked shut. *Whew!* The guinea pigs were safe, but now I had a very depressed snake on my hands—uh, paws.

I looked up at Bobby's glass box. How was I going to get him back up there? "Bob, my boy, as long as you're a library snake, you won't be hunting your own food. Especially since Robin is feeding you dead mice."

That was the wrong thing to say. Bobby curled himself into a tight coil and hid his head in the middle.

Too bad Alice wasn't here. She would've known what to do. I looked over my shoulder at the guinea pigs. They'd poked their noses out of their hut, but weren't coming any closer.

"He's turned into a monster," squeaked Pearl.

"Not a monster," I said. "He's just figured out how snakes are supposed to act." I nudged the snake with my nose. "Come on, fella. You need to get back where you belong before Robin finds you out here."

Behind me, the pigs started chittering to each other. Then Posha said, "We've changed our minds about the deal."

I swung my head around. "What? What deal?"

"The deal we made with you." Posha crept a little closer to the wire. "We can't let you go home while there's a monster running loose."

I flattened my ears. "He's not a monster," I repeated. "Just a confused snake."

"Whatever." Pearl came forward, too. "Now that we know he's dangerous, we need a bodyguard."

I huffed. "Briggston will be back. He can be your bodyguard."

The pigs looked at each other and broke out into shrill squeaks. "Ha!" said Pearl. "Briggston can't run half as fast as you, even without a hurt leg."

"And he doesn't have any front claws," added Posha.

I sat a little straighter. It was nice to be acknowledged for my superior skills. But then I frowned. "I can't stay. The farm is falling to pieces without me. You and Briggston will have to work something out. Or maybe you'll just have to stay inside your cage where you're safe."

The rodents looked at each other again. They had a gleam in their eyes I didn't care for.

"No deal," squeaked Posha. "Not until the snake is gone." They scrambled back inside their hut before I could think of a suitable retort.

Great. I snagged the carpet with my claws and ripped a few threads loose before jabbing at the snake with my stick leg. "Now look what you've done. Why couldn't you have stayed in your glass box where you belong?"

Bobby Scales poked his head out from underneath a coil. "The book ssssaysssss I don't belong in a box."

"Well..." I didn't have a comeback for that.

"You want to be free and back at your farm, and the guinea pigsssss want to be free of their cage. Sssso why can't I be free, too?"

I sat down and scratched my ear with a back paw. The reptile had a point. Why should the rest of us be happy and expect him to stay cooped up inside a little box? "I don't know, Bob. That's a tough one. I just know that sometimes you have to use some self control to keep yourself out of trouble. That's why I'm not chasing the guinea pigs myself."

"But you'll chasssse critterssss when you get home, right?"

"Yeah, hopefully. Now that you've messed up the deal, though, I may be stuck here forever." My whiskers drooped along with my head.

"Jusssst like me." Bobby's coils loosened. He laid his head across my back, and we sat that way for a while, each pondering thoughts of freedom, I suppose.

Suddenly he reared up. "I have an idea!"

My head stayed down. If I knew anything about snakes, it was that they didn't have much of a brain to think up ideas. "Yeah? What?"

"You could take me with you!" Bobby's head was weaving from side to side now. "You have sssssnakessss on the farm, right?"

I grunted.

"I could become part of the ssssnake community."

My whiskers twitched. "Uh, Bob—there's not much of a community. Snakes usually like to hang out by themselves. Besides that, you have a pretty fancy spread here." I nodded toward his box. "You might not appreciate living in a hole in the pasture. It gets pretty cold in the winter."

"Don't you get cold in the winter?"

"Yeah, but I'm used to it. I grow a little more fur and eat a few more kibbles, and I'm all set."

Bobby's eyes narrowed. I could almost see the gears turning in his tiny brain. "Ssssnakessss don't have fur."

"No." I shook my head. "The snakes I know burrow down into their holes and sleep all winter. Kinda boring if you ask me."

Bobby Scales started swaying again. "No. I could do it. I could! Take me with you. Pleasssse."

His back and forth movements were getting a little mesmerizing. I blinked to clear my head. "Listen, there's no way. It's not like I can just open the door and invite you to stroll across town with me."

"Let me hide in Robin'ssss bag with you."

I had a sudden image of being cozied up next to a snake in a small, dark place. The fur on one of my shoulders began to poof, and I quickly licked it back in place. "Uh, I hate to tell you this, but I don't think there's room in the bag for both of us."

"I have an idea!" Posha's voice made me jump. I looked around and saw just the tip of her nose poking out of the hut.

Great. Here I was, chief in charge of security, reduced to taking ideas from reptiles and rodents. I flicked my tail and licked my shoulder again, giving myself time to control my words. "Okay," I said finally. "So what's your idea?"

"Let's put the snake in the bag instead of you."

Now *all* of my fur poofed. "And leave me here?" This was the worst idea ever.

Posha rumbled. "No, we'll convince Robin to take you along dressed in costume like us."

"No way." I sprang to my feet. "I will absolutely, positively *not* put on some frilly costume and have everyone in the neighborhood laugh at me. Never again." I stalked off toward my basket.

"Then the deal is off!" Posha called after me. "You don't take the snake, you don't go either."

I was so mad I felt like shredding a few pages of one of the books on the floor. Instead, I hopped into my basket and shredded the edge of the blanket, then poked my nose under my tail to shut out the library and everything inside it. Maybe this was all a bad dream. Maybe I would wake up any moment and find myself back at the farm dealing with less exasperating problems—like keeping Old Mangy out of the farmyard.

I could only wish.

15

FLYING BOOKS AND OTHER DISCOVERIES

Bobby had returned to his glass box before Robin arrived the next morning. She didn't seem to notice the turned up corner on its cover. She was only at the library long enough to feed the guinea pigs and fill my bowl with kibbles.

I watched her from my basket, trying to understand the change in routine. After she left, I decided to ask the guinea pigs what was going on. And while I was at it, I could try persuading them to change their minds about the snake, too.

Posha and Pearl were at their food dish, gorging themselves on the orange slices Robin had given them.

"Hey," I said.

They kept eating, not even bothering to look my way.

"Hey," I said again.

Still no response.

"If you two won't even say 'hi' to me, I might as well just open your cage and let the snake inside for a nice conversation." Not that I would actually do that, but it sure got their attention.

They rushed to the wire door and put their front paws against it, like they might try holding it closed if I gave it a tug. "You wouldn't dare," Pearl said.

I sat. "Good morning to you, too."

The rodents looked at each other. "What do you want?" Posha asked. "Have you come to tell us you've changed your mind?"

"No. I just wanted to know why Robin didn't stick around this morning."

"Oh, that." Pearl gave herself a little shake and turned back to the food bowl. "It's Sunday," she said, talking around another orange slice.

"Sunday?" I'd never heard the word before.

"Yeah. That's the day the library is closed."

I rubbed my whiskers and thought about that. I didn't much like the idea of being left alone with the rodents inside this empty, boring space. Even being forced to go to story time with a bunch of noisy kids was better than having no human company at all. "Oka-a-a-ay," I said. "So how often does a Sunday happen?"

Posha tilted her head and looked at me while she chewed a bit of orange. "Anyone who *reads* would know that Sunday only happens once a week—once every seven days."

Great. I wasn't just left alone with rodents. I was left alone with *stuck-up* rodents. I took a deep breath and forced my claws to stay sheathed. "And there are humans here every day except Sunday?"

"Usually." Posha nodded. "Sometimes there are special days when the library is closed, though. Like Tuesday, when Robin's taking us to the fair."

Pearl pulled the last chunk of orange out of the dish. "Are you getting into costume to come with us?"

"No way—" I began. But then Posha grabbed Pearl's orange slice.

Pearl wouldn't let go, and soon they were jerking the piece back and forth like a game of tug of war. Then the piece broke in two, and the rodents' game changed to a race—each one gobbling her chunk down at top speed.

Good grief. It was no use trying to reason with them while they were eating. I stalked to my basket and had almost fallen back to sleep when a sudden loud *thunk* made my eyes snap open. I heard another *thunk*, then another. Peering around the side of the desk, I tried to spot the source of the noise. All at once I saw a book fly *right through* the brick wall beside the glass door. It fell into a tall box sitting directly underneath with yet another *thunk*.

I hissed and jumped backwards, knowing enough about books to realize that they weren't supposed to jump through solid walls. I waited for a few swishes of my very poofed tail, but no more books appeared. The room settled back to silence.

Maybe I needed to investigate. If books could leap through the wall, maybe I could too. I padded over to the tall box and examined it. It smelled strongly of paper and glue, just like the rest of the library. If only I could see what was inside…

I backed up a couple of paces, gathered my legs under me, and sprang to the top of the box. My three good legs scrabbled for a foothold, fighting with my stick leg, which was trying its hardest to send me back to the ground. Luckily, the three good legs prevailed.

When I'd steadied myself, I looked down into the box. Several books lay at the bottom. No surprise there. I carefully worked my way around the edge of the box and sniffed at the wall where the books had come through. The brick wall wasn't solid in that spot, but had a metal plate with a flap, sort of like the cat flap Felix uses to go into and out of his humans' house. A cat flap! A way out!

I poked my paw through the flap—and realized that the opening was much skinnier than I was. My whiskers drooped with disappointment. A mouse might be able to scramble through, or maybe Bobby Scales. But certainly not a muscular, well-developed guy like me.

With my paw holding the flap open, I could feel the fresh air wafting over my face, carrying the scent of green grass and sunshine. Oh, if only I was out there frisking on the lawn—well, more like stumbling with my stick leg. But stumbling was preferable to sitting, and I'd been doing way too much of that lately.

I jumped down from the box and sat beside the glass door. A squirrel was jumping from limb to limb in a tree across the street. I wished I was free again, just like that squirrel. I wished that I was back at the farm where I belonged. I wished I was doing morning report with Pauline or stalking grasshoppers in the garden with Kid or even arguing with Felix on the porch about who was going to do barn patrol. *Anything* would be better than sitting inside this quiet, mouse-free place.

I went back to bed and slept until evening, when I returned to the door and pressed my nose against the glass. I was in such a stupor that I almost didn't notice the flicker of movement outside, between the bench and the brick wall. My eyes focused and I sprang to my feet.

Alice!

She and I rubbed faces with the pane of glass between us. Her mouth moved, but I couldn't hear what she was saying. She scratched at the door with her paw—not that I could hear that either.

My whiskers spronged and my fur felt so twitchy that if one of the guinea pigs had started squeaking right then, I would've achieved liftoff and hit the ceiling. How could I get to her? How could I talk with her? She might have something super important to tell me—a way I might be able to escape this place without the guinea pigs' help.

I paced back and forth in front of the door until I was

a whirlwind of poofed fur and unsheathed claws. Suddenly my head whapped against something so hard I saw stars, and it wasn't the kind starting to glow in the darkening sky, if you know what I mean.

When my vision cleared, I realized I'd run right into the book box I'd explored earlier in the day. The book box, and…

…the flap!

The book flap! It wasn't big enough to let me out or let Alice in, but if I climbed on the box and she scrambled onto the bench outside, maybe we could hear each other through the opening.

I leaped onto the box and almost fell head first onto the pile of books inside. I steadied myself with my good legs, then used my stick leg to jiggle the flap. "Alice!" I called through the narrow opening and waited for a few whisker twitches. "Alice!"

Finally, I heard a bit of scrambling outside. Then a white paw shot through the open flap and wiggled, looking for all the world like the brick wall had just grown a cat foot. I almost fell backward into the book box.

I balanced myself again. "Alice, can you hear me?"

"Loud and clear. Can you hear me?"

I nodded, then remembered she couldn't see me. "Yup. I can hear fine. Just having a little trouble standing here." I was teetering back and forth, struggling to keep my grip.

"Guess we'll have to keep it short, then," came Alice's voice. "Are you all set for your ride to the fair?"

My tail gave a violent flick that almost sent me over the edge. Might as well get right to the point. "Uh, Alice, there's been a change of plans. I might not be able to travel to the fair with the guinea pigs after all. I need your help thinking up another idea—or else I might be stuck in this library forever."

16

CORNERED INTO COMPROMISE

At my bad news, Alice's white paw twitched in the slot. "What's happened? Why can't you go?"

I huffed. "Because Bobby Scales decided to start acting like a real snake instead of a pampered pet. He attacked the guinea pigs last night, and now the rodents won't help me unless I take him along."

"Oh." She went silent for a moment. "You *could* bring him. Emma wouldn't mind."

My ears flattened, not that Alice could see. "It's not a matter of Emma minding. It's a matter of logistics. I can't just hop in a bag with a snake and expect Robin not to notice. One of us might sneak out that way, but not both of us."

"Oh." That seemed to be Alice's favorite response of the day.

"Did you have any luck persuading Briggston?" If the cat had been stubborn about the plan, my problems with the snake weren't going to matter anyway.

"It's been a little tricky." Alice's voice wavered. "He wasn't opposed to dressing up and entering the contest, especially since he wants to get back to 'civilization,' as he calls it. But getting Lil and Emma to do their part has been a challenge."

"You can't get them to take Briggston to the fair? I thought you could convince them to do *anything*."

"I don't speak human, George. I'm good at persuading, but not interjecting completely new information. Like, let's dress up the cat and take him to the fair."

"Huh." I pondered for a moment. "I think I might have an idea for that. Wait right there."

I leaped off the edge of the box—well, more like did a nose dive—and hustled over to the guinea pig cage. They were sitting beside their food bowl, not moving a muscle. I would've guessed they were napping except their eyes were wide open. Come to think of it, I'd never seen them with their eyes shut. Maybe the critters never slept.

"Hey, girls!" I said.

Both of them jumped and wood shavings went flying. "Don't wake us up like that," squeaked Pearl.

"Wake? But you... Never mind. I have an important favor to ask."

Posha raised her nose. "What's that?"

"I need to borrow your scrap of newspaper that tells about the fair."

Pearl rumbled. "Why would you want that? Have you figured out how to read?"

"No, but humans can," I said. "Alice is having trouble informing my human about the pet show. If Emma saw the newspaper article, maybe she'd take the hint."

The pigs put their noses together and grumbled and rumbled a while. Pearl finally looked back at me. "Why do you want Briggston to be at the fair if you're not going?"

My tail started to flick. Alice would be wondering what was taking so long. "I'll figure out a way to the fair later. Right now I need the article."

Pearl settled onto the wood chips. "First tell us how you're going to get there *with* the snake. Then we'll give you the newspaper article."

I laid back my ears. "I'm working on it, okay? I'll think of something."

"Uh, uh." Posha put her paws on the wire. "You're probably trying to think of a way to escape that doesn't include taking the snake. You turned him into a monster. You need to take him with you. If we don't have that guarantee, we're not helping."

They both scuttled into their hut.

I felt like opening the cage and raking the two of them out with my claws, but that would definitely make them even more upset and contrary. I needed some advice on how to sweet talk stubborn rodents, and luckily my advisor on sweet talking was standing just outside. I limped back across the library, jumped back onto the big box, and slid my paw through the book slot. "Alice?"

Her whiskers peeked through. "Yes? Did you figure something out?"

"The guinea pigs have that newspaper article that tells about the fair. I hoped they could lend it to you."

"Oh! That would be perfect! I could leave it somewhere for Lil to find."

"Yeah, that's what I thought, too. There's just one problem." I lowered my voice and leaned as close as I could to the slot. "The guinea pigs won't give it to me until I agree to their plan. But I can't take the snake with me—like I said, there's only room in the bag for one of us. So … any ideas on how to get the rodents to cooperate?"

Alice went silent. Maybe she couldn't think of a way to get those critters to help, either. "Alice, this fair idea is just not going to work. Let's go to Plan B. Maybe if you could distract Robin when she's leaving tomorrow night, I could slip outside and—"

"But that would leave Briggston at the farm."

My whiskers went rigid. "I don't have a better idea," I growled. "Briggston can probably stay with Lil if she likes him so much."

"But he won't be able to get home. He misses his friends at the library."

"And I miss my friends back on the farm. I need to get

home, Alice, before everything falls apart. You said that yourself."

Another pause. My tail flicked, once, twice, thrice, waiting for Alice to say something, waiting for her to figure out I was right.

The flap wiggled as Alice's paw tapped against it from the other side. Then it went still. "What's the guinea pigs' plan?" she asked.

"What?"

"You said the guinea pigs weren't cooperating until you agreed to their plan. Does that only mean taking the snake with you, or is there something else?"

Rats. I'd been hoping to avoid that topic. "No, taking the snake was just part of it. They want me to dress up in costume so I don't need to go in the bag. Then there's room for Bobby. Obviously *that's* not going to happen."

"Why not? Sounds like a good idea to me. It'd make you easier to switch with Briggston, too."

My fur poofed again. Why did I even bother to flatten it? "I am *not* going to be the laughing stock of the farm."

Alice's paw waved in the slot until it found my nose. She patted me. "Calm down, George. The critters on the farm won't even know you've dressed up. I won't tell them."

"But there will be other animals at the fair who'll definitely see me. Word gets around. Being dressed up like a pink princess by Emma's niece was even more humiliating than losing Emma's flock of chickens to a skunk raid."

"Then don't be a princess. What are the guinea pigs going as?"

"Pirates, cheerleaders, something like that."

"So not princesses. What would *you* like to be?"

The lion came to mind. He'd looked pretty tough, even after being shrunk and flattened. "I don't want—"

"Duty is duty, George. Isn't that what you always say?"

I didn't have a response for that one.

"Well?" Alice prodded me with her paw.

"Fine," I huffed. "I'll see what I can do. Wait right there."

I limped my way back to the guinea pigs' cage. The rodents were back outside the hut. They saw me coming and started chittering to each other.

I plopped down in front of them. "Fine," I said. "I'll get dressed up. But only if I get to be a lion."

Pearl grumbled a bit and stuck her nose in the air, but Posha nipped her shoulder. "We can try. Sometimes humans don't understand very well."

"But I wanted to be a *cheerleader,* Posh, not something big and clunky like a lion."

Posha nipped her again. "You want the snake gone or not?"

Pearl glared at her, glared at me, then waddled into the hut—hopefully to retrieve the scrap of paper.

I shifted from one paw to the other. When Pearl did finally appear with the newspaper, I practically ripped it in two grabbing it. "Thanks," I mumbled, paper between teeth, before I hobbled back to the book box. My three good legs were getting a little wobbly from all this jumping up and down.

"Alice!" I stuck my paw through the slot and called as best as I could with a mouth full of paper. There was a long pause. My heart thudded to a stop. Had she already left?

"I'm here." Alice's voice was a bit breathless as her paw appeared next to mine. "Some humans came by, and I had to hide under the bench. Didn't want to get chased off."

"Right," I said, mumbling around my mouthful of wet paper. "Good thinking." I steadied my body against the wall and thrust the paper toward the slot. "Here it comes!"

Alice's paw almost scratched my nose as she grappled in the air. Her claws finally connected with the paper.

The paper and paw disappeared. The slot snapped closed.

I spat out the bitter taste of pulpy, half-dissolved newsprint and pushed open the slot again. "Did you get it?"

"Got it," she said. Her words were muffled, like she wasn't very close. "It dropped on the ground, but I'm standing on it."

"Great," I said. "You know what to do."

"You, too." Alice's voice floated up to me. "See you at the fair!"

"See you."

I hopped down from the box and shuffled over to the glass door. Alice was padding away from the library with the scrap of paper dangling from her mouth. I waved my tail but she didn't see me.

Hopefully this crazy plan would work.

17

DUTY IS DUTY

A mob of kids attended story time the next day, wiggling around on their pillows and chattering like overexcited squirrels about choosing the rodents' costumes. I was sorely tempted to disappear until the hubbub was over, but that wouldn't help me get home—and duty was duty, as Alice had reminded me.

I sauntered around the story corner and greeted each kid with a rub on the leg. They all patted me and one of the boys even scratched between my ears, which felt pretty good. Maybe I should've been doing this petting tour all along. Too late for that, though, because tomorrow I was going home.

When it looked like everyone had arrived, I hopped on top of the rodents' cage, waving my tail like a flag in order to get everyone's attention. Then I leaped to the top of the bookshelf where Robin was keeping the guinea pigs' costumes and photos.

"Lookit Briggston!" one of the kids squealed.

I tried to keep from cringing at that high, squeaky voice. Instead, I nudged the pile of costumes until I found the furry ruff that'd been around Pearl's neck the day the rodents had been dressed up as lions. The scrap of fluff was too small to fit around my own muscular neck, but I managed to nose it around until it was perched on one of my ears.

I sat down on the shelf with my nose in the air. Not that I was trying to look haughty—even though the lion in the animal encyclopedia *had* looked pretty proud of himself. I just needed to keep the scrap of fur balanced on my ear.

"Lookit Briggston!" the little kid said again.

All eyes fixed on me. I forced myself to sit still. Then one kid started to giggle, and suddenly they were all laughing and pointing.

My whiskers went rigid. It was an effort to keep my ears from flattening and disturbing the fake lion ruff balanced there. I wanted to jump off the shelf and skedaddle back to my basket as fast as I could.

Duty is duty, I kept telling myself. Duty is duty.

I could see Pearl and Posha poking their noses through the wire of their cage. Posha gave me a nod, like she was trying to encourage me.

Robin strode into the corner with her mouth set into a

straight line—the closest I'd ever seen her come to frowning. "Kids, kids," she said. "Remember, we use quiet voices in the library."

"Lookit Briggston!" Maybe those were the only words that little boy knew. This time he pointed at me.

Uh, oh.

I stood up, preparing to turn on some kitty charm so Robin would let me stay.

"Briggston wants a costume, too." A girl popped up from her spot on the floor and came toward me. She took the fur off my ear and wrapped it around my good paw instead. Then she sorted through the pile and found the matching ruff Posha had worn.

By that time, the entire crowd of kids had gathered around me. The second ruff went on my stick leg. Then a tiny pirate hat was hung from my ear and a cheerleader pom pom was attached to my tail. It was all I could do to keep standing there, tall and proud, knowing how ridiculous I must look with guinea pig-sized costumes dangling off every part of me.

Robin finally intervened. She cut through the swarm of small bodies, laughing. "Okay, okay, kids. Poor Briggston needs some room to breathe!" She started shooing the kids back to their places.

"Can Briggston go to the fair, too?" a boy asked.

"Can we make him match the guinea pigs?" a girl pleaded.

"He could be an extra big cheerleader!" another girl shouted, jumping up and down.

My ears *did* flatten this time, and a pirate hat fell to the ground.

"Whoa!" Robin held up her hands. "Quiet down, kids. This is a library, remember."

That set off a wave of shushes. The kids got somewhat quieter, although there was still plenty of whispering.

Robin returned to the shelf where I was standing and stroked my back. "Are you really wanting to get dressed up, Briggston? That would be a first."

I rubbed my face against her hand and tried to look suitably excited.

She shook her head. "You're full of surprises, cat." She looked back at the kids. "I guess Briggston wants to go, too."

A chorus of cheers went up, quickly hushed by Robin's finger against her lips. "Let's take a look at the photos of Posha and Pearl and vote on them first," she said. "And then we'll think up a matching costume for Briggston."

Great. Just great. I waved my good paw in the air, hoping that seeing the lion fur might influence the masses. No one was looking at me now, though. They were all focused on the photos in Robin's hands.

"Okay," Robin said. "We dressed Posha and Pearl as pirates, cheerleaders, lions, and cowboys." She held up all the photos. "You only get to vote for one. Do you know which one is your favorite?"

"The pirates!" said a pipsqueak in the front row.

Robin smiled at him. "Wait until I say your choice and then raise your hand." She looked out over the crowd. "Here we go. Who wants cheerleaders?"

Only three girls raised their hands. *Whew*. I escaped that humiliation at least.

"Pirates?"

A group of boys raised their hands plus a couple of little girls in the front row.

"Lions?"

I stood and waved my paw in the air again, trying my best to look regal and proud like the lion in the book. Some of the girls giggled and pointed at me, but only one of them raised her hand. I waved my tail in the air to get more attention, but Robin had already moved on.

"Cowboys?"

This time a mob of hands shot into the air.

Robin was counting under her breath and when she finished, she smiled. "We have a winner. It was a close race between pirates and cowboys, but cowboys have won."

Another chorus of cheers. The three girls who'd wanted cheerleaders were all sitting with big frowns on their faces, but the rest of the crowd seemed happy enough.

"Posha and Pearl can be the cowboys, and Briggston can be their horse!" A skinny little guy with dark hair hanging in his eyes spoke up.

Great. I almost stuck my tail between my legs, just like

Brutus and Festus at home when they're upset. To be seen in public with a pair of rodents on my back… My reputation would be in tatters. I scrambled down the shelf to the guinea pigs' cage. Both Posha and Pearl were looking disgruntled, too.

"Imagine," Posha said when she saw me. "Choosing cowboys over pirates."

"And cowboys aren't nearly as cute as cheerleaders," Pearl added. "The judges will pass us by for sure."

I watched as the kids took the guinea pigs out of their cage and dressed them up in their cowboy costumes. Then I dug in my claws and forced myself to stay put as the kids placed both of the critters on my back. Guinea pigs, in case you didn't know, have very scratchy feet.

"Stop digging in your heels," I hissed to Pearl.

"I'll fall off otherwise," she squeaked back.

My ears flattened and thoughts of fresh rodent for supper flashed through my mind, but I managed to keep my claws under control.

The guinea pig claws didn't hurt so much after I'd been given a little blanket for a saddle. But then someone attached stringy brown yarn to my own handsome orange tail, and fastened some onto my head and my neck as well. The yarn on my tail made me jump every time it swished against my legs, and the yarn on my head fell into my face when I looked down. Definitely not the best outfit to wear during an escape.

"Good job, everyone," Robin said. "We have this

figured out. Let's take off the costumes and pack them away for tomorrow. Whoever wants to help dress Briggston and the guinea pigs for the contest can meet me at the fairgrounds tomorrow morning."

The kids cheered and jumped around and *finally* removed the swishy yarn from my head and tail. Unfortunately they were going to torture me with it again tomorrow.

What had I gotten myself into?

18

PLANS AND MORE PLANS

Later that day I sat in my basket, licking a bunch of scratches on my back caused by rodent toenails and wishing I'd never agreed to this humiliating plan. My costume had been folded and set on the bookshelf in the story corner within easy reach of my claws. I was tempted to hop up there and shred the awful thing, but I knew that would completely ruin tomorrow's plans.

I was so busy working on the prickly spots that I almost didn't notice Robin walk toward the front door with her big bag slung over her shoulder. I stopped in mid lick and hustled after her. Good thing, too, because I could see Alice crouched under the bench outside.

As Robin opened the door, I made a feint in her direction.

"Stay right there, you crazy cat," she said, looking at

me instead of behind her where Alice was slinking inside like a silent black shadow.

I crouched like I might make a break for freedom, which kept Robin's eyes fixed on me while she slipped out the door. I padded closer and sat beside the glass until Robin had climbed into her car and driven off down the street.

"All clear," I said.

Alice stepped out from her hiding spot on a bottom shelf, sat down next to me, and began licking my shoulder. "Good grief, George. Your fur is sticking up like you've been rubbed the wrong way with a balloon."

"I *feel* like I've been rubbed the wrong way with a balloon," I growled. "Try prancing around a crowd of humans with two rodents stuck on your back. And it'll be a bigger crowd tomorrow."

"Poor George." Alice gave a few more licks. "So your part of the plan is under control?"

"I think so. Robin is taking me along, fully costumed. I just need to coach the snake on how to get in the bag. He may require a little help." I scratched another itchy spot on my back. "How about you?"

She frowned. "Well, Emma found the article I left on Ted's work bench in the shed—and she *did* decide to enter the pet show."

"That's great!"

"But she's entering Pauline, not Briggston."

"What?" My ears shot straight up. "Why Pauline?"

"Probably because Pauline's around and Briggston isn't. The cat's hiding in Lil's house, after all."

"Great." I dug my claws into the carpet. "*Now* what are we going to do?"

She rubbed an ear. "Felix and I are trying to convince Briggston to sneak into Pauline's trailer tomorrow morning and go along. But he claims that he hates the prickly feel of gravel under his toes. And wide open spaces scare him silly."

I had visions of Briggston refusing to set foot outside Lil's door. Then I'd be stuck parading around in a costume with guinea pigs on my back, all for nothing. "Can you get the dogs to help? Some canine encouragement might be just the thing."

"They'll do what they can. It'll be tricky to get an unwilling cat across the yard and into the trailer without being seen. Kid gave the hounds some ideas about being sneaky that she said she learned from you."

"Oh." I sat up a little straighter. "And what about you?"

"I won't be at the farm tomorrow because Twila is taking me straight to the fair to watch the show. I'll wander around and try to find you. Pauline thinks the large animals will be in a different place than the small ones, and I'm not going to roust Briggston out of the trailer until I know where to take him. Then I'll help him get into place, we'll make the switch, and you and I will skedaddle back to Pauline's trailer."

Alice gave her own shoulder a swipe with her tongue. She *was* looking a little more ruffled than usual.

"Sounds good," I said, nodding. "I'll be ready and waiting. The sooner the better. In fact, if you can get Briggston in place early enough, he can be the one to play horse for the rodents. Oh, and you'd better warn Pauline that I'm coming with a snake so she doesn't get spooked when we arrive."

I looked over toward the story corner, wondering if I should give Bobby some tips on subterfuge. Snakes are usually pretty good at moving around unnoticed, but slipping through tall grass is a little different from hiding in the midst of a pack of humans.

"George." Alice nudged me. "I was wondering, how are you going to get out of your pet carrier?"

"Huh?" I'd been thinking about snakes and Pauline, not pet carriers. I scrubbed at my whiskers. "Oh, that. I don't think it'll be a problem. I'm figuring Robin will use the carrier for the two rodents, and she won't want to stuff me inside with them. I'll probably just sit in the front seat, like you do with Twila when she takes you to the farm."

Alice tilted her head. "I don't know, George. Going to a strange place with lots of humans isn't quite the same as Twila taking me to the farm. Robin might not trust you to stay out of trouble."

"I'll be picture perfect all morning while she's getting us ready," I said. "I won't give her any reason to worry."

Alice's whiskers twitched. "I'm sure you won't."

121

I bristled. "It'll be fine. You take care of Briggston, and I'll take care of things here."

"Yes, sir," said Alice. There was still a hint of a laugh in her voice, but I ignored it. I wasn't in the mood to be growly because I was finally going home.

Freedom, here I come!

19

THE BEST LAID PLANS ...

I spent the rest of the night working with Bobby on how to slither unseen around the books on the top shelf by his glass box. It would've been better to have him practice on the floor—more open spaces, after all. But the guinea pigs were insistent that he stay out of their territory.

I also coached the rodents on the best way to squeal and run around their cage to provide a cover for Bobby's escape.

When morning came, Alice and I sat by the glass door, waiting for Robin to arrive. "See you soon," Alice said, when we saw her car coming around the corner. Alice crouched behind some books on the book shelf, and I provided a diversion for her to slip out unseen.

I noted with relief that Robin had brought her large purple bag. It would've been a disaster if she'd decided to switch to a smaller bag just for the day. I followed her over to the circulation desk and crunched some kibbles while she disappeared into her office. By the time she returned with the pet carrier, most of the kibbles were in my belly.

I shivered with anticipation. Leaving the rest of the kibbles, I trotted after her toward the guinea pigs' cage. As I passed the circulation desk, I looked up. Oh, no! Her bag was still there. Wasn't she going to take it with her?

I dashed over to the story corner. Robin put the pet carrier down and opened the door. "Don't worry, Briggs. I'm not forgetting you, but I don't trust you to ride with the pigs."

Fine. Great. I figured that'd be the case. *But what about the bag? What about Bobby?*

Robin took the costumes from the bookshelf and laid them on top of the carrier. My fur went into instant poof. She wasn't going to put them in her big bag. She wasn't planning to take the bag along!

I jumped onto the carrier, batted the costumes to the floor, and stretched out on top. Now she'd *have* to take the bag.

Robin glanced at me and shook her head. "Briggston, it'll be your fault if I forget to put those costumes into my bag. Get off of there, you crazy cat." She scooted me onto the floor, replaced the costumes, and opened the guinea pigs' cage.

Well, at least she planned on taking the bag. But it was still on her desk, clear across the room. If the bag wasn't coming to the snake, the snake would have to go to the bag. It would be no problem for him to crawl across the room, but how was he going to get up onto the desk? He didn't have springy legs like I did.

There wasn't time to worry about that now. I had to get the snake moving! I slunk around the corner to the back side of Bobby's box. He was coiled and ready to go, his attention fixed on Robin and the guinea pigs. "Psst!" I said. "It's time!"

He jerked around, looked down and saw me. "But... the bag?"

"No time to explain. Just get down here!"

If snakes had shoulders, I'm sure he would've shrugged. But he nosed the cover aside and slithered out. Then he started crawling along the shelf, heading toward the wall instead of plopping down onto the pillows stacked below his cage, like I expected. Maybe he'd misunderstood me.

"You have to come down!" I hissed. "Go the other way."

Bobby put an extra wiggle in his glide. "No worriessss," he said. "I know what I'm doing." He reached the wall and started slithering down the cracks between the bricks.

He was crawling down the wall!

My mouth fell open. It hit me that I'd never actually *seen* him get down from the shelf. I figured that he'd jumped down, like me. But he could climb! I gaped at him until he slid onto the floor. He glided over and gave me a shove with his head. "Now what?"

I closed my mouth. "You're brilliant," I said. "You just solved a very big problem." I limped back to Robin's desk with the snake slithering behind me. We'd just reached the wall behind the desk when Robin picked up the carrier with the guinea pigs and started walking toward us.

"Get under cover," I told him. "If you have a chance, crawl up onto the desk. The bag's on top."

Robin reached the desk just as Bobby slipped behind my basket. I bounded toward her, hoping to draw her attention.

"You're super excited, aren't you, Briggs?" Robin laughed. "Well, it's your turn next."

She placed the pet carrier with the guinea pigs on her desk, put the costumes in her bag, and walked back to her office.

"Now!" I signaled to Bobby.

He wiggled out and started crawling up the cracks in the brick wall, slithering for all he was worth. Inside the carrier, Pearl and Posha were watching him with bug eyes. Pearl started to squeal, "He's coming after us!"

Robin's voice came from her office. "Briggston, what are you doing?"

Figures. I always get the blame.

"Be quiet, idiot," I hissed at the pig. "He's not after you."

But the damage had already been done. I heard

Robin's footsteps coming from her office. Well, if she was going to blame me anyway, I'd give her something to look at. I took a running leap and caught the edge of the desktop with my good front paw. I scrambled and pushed with my back legs until I heaved myself up.

Bobby was in plain sight, still slithering up the wall. He was almost even with the top of the desk, but not quite. Both guinea pigs were staring at him.

I pushed my face against the slats of their carrier. "He's headed for the bag. Don't let Robin know he's there or he'll be staying and I'll be leaving."

Posha tore her eyes away from the snake and looked at me. She was just about ready to say something when Robin arrived.

"Briggston! What are you doing?"

I started rubbing against the cage door and purring.

Robin huffed, then laughed. "I didn't know you could jump so high. Especially with a hurt leg." She rubbed my head. "You're quite the cat."

Then she did something truly terrifying. She lifted another pet carrier onto the desk. "I borrowed this one especially for you, Briggs. Look, it's even got a blanket inside. First class accommodations."

She reached over to grab me. I bristled and considered jumping off the desk and disappearing behind a bookshelf. But out of the corner of my eye, I saw Bobby's head disappear into Robin's bag. The rest of his body was still exposed.

I started rubbing against Robin's arm, adjusting the volume of my purr so that the entire desk started vibrating. Anything to keep her eyes on me.

"You're such a good cat," Robin said. She picked me up and put me into the carrier.

I thought about yowling and clawing and creating a fuss. Anything to get out of that carrier! But the tip of Bobby's tail was just vanishing into the bag. He was ready to go. The guinea pigs were ready to go. I couldn't cause a commotion and risk getting left behind.

The latch on the carrier door clunked into place. From my spot inside, I couldn't see how Robin had fastened it, and I wouldn't be able to reach it anyway.

Trapped again.

20

PROBLEMS AND MORE PROBLEMS

The guinea pigs and I rode in the back seat of Robin's car on the way to the fair. I stared through the slats of the pet carrier at the seat ahead of me where Robin's bag was sitting. There'd been a tense moment in the library when Robin had picked up the bag and commented on how heavy it seemed. Thankfully she hadn't taken the time to rummage through it, though. Bobby hadn't been discovered—yet.

The problem was, now that I was inside this carrier I couldn't get close enough to Bobby to advise him. I hoped he had the sense to get out of the bag before Robin needed to dig out our costumes. And I hoped he had the sense to find a different hiding spot until Alice came looking for us. If he got excited and tried to make a break for it on his own, he might be caught by some human who didn't like snakes as much as Robin did. I should've warned him sooner about the dangers of the human world.

And that wasn't my only worry. Now that I was locked inside a carrier, I wouldn't be able to slip out of sight and let Briggston reclaim his role of library cat as soon as he and Alice found me. Our plan was seriously falling apart!

I unsheathed my claws and frazzled my blanket until Robin slowed the car and brought it to a stop. Then I plastered my face against the slats of my cage and meowed piteously as she got out and opened the back door. Maybe she'd feel sorry for me and take me out right here, right now.

Instead, she took hold of the carrier with the guinea pigs. "Be right back for you, Briggs," she said, and pushed the door shut again.

Great. So much for my powers of persuasion. But at least I was alone with Bobby now. "Psst! Bob!"

"Yeah?" Bobby's head peeked around the car seat.

"Don't get out of the bag yet!" I had visions of him slipping out of the car when Robin opened the door, then wandering around town until some slavering dog with sharp teeth spotted him. "Wait until we're inside and I give you the signal, okay? Then you'll need to hustle out of there and find a different hiding spot until Alice arrives."

Bobby glanced toward the door, swaying slightly as

though trying to decide whether to take orders from me or not. "Fine," he said finally, and disappeared from view.

None too soon. Robin was back again. She opened the front door and pulled out her bag. Since she didn't squeal or yell anything about an escaped snake, I figured Bobby must've gotten himself under cover in time. Then she took me out of the back. "Okay, Briggs. You be on your best behavior now. You're representing the kids at the library, you know, and that's quite a responsibility."

I crouched down on the tatters of my blanket. I hadn't thought about the situation quite like that before. It was my *responsibility* to make my best effort for the kids. And here I was planning to run out on them. How could I carry out my duty to the farm and my responsibility to the kids at the same time? This was becoming way too complicated.

When Robin walked into the building with me, I could hear lots of other animals. Meows, yaps, squeaks, squawks. I laid back my ears and all thoughts of responsibility vanished. I couldn't wait for Robin to open the carrier so I could skedaddle.

Robin set me down on a long table in the middle of a line of other pet carriers, put her bag down on the table beside it, and left. The guinea pigs were in the carrier next to mine, and Posha was peering through the slats in the side. "You okay?"

"I've been better."

"Probably should get your fur under control or Robin might decide to leave you in there."

I looked down. Posha was right. My fur was sticking out in all directions, and I hadn't even felt it poof. Too much racket and distraction. I started to lick my tail.

"George!"

I looked down, and there was Alice.

"Alice!" I said, "What a relief! You need to get Briggston over here ASAP."

"Uh, George," she said. "About that—I'm afraid we have a small problem."

"Another one?" My tail poofed again, and I pressed my face against the wire door of the carrier. "What's wrong?"

"Briggston refuses to leave Pauline's trailer. I guess the dogs had a terrible time convincing him to come out of the house this morning. Pauline said that Brutus ended up carrying him to the trailer by the scruff of his neck because he was twitching so badly he couldn't walk. He didn't calm down on the ride to town, either, and now that there's only me to coax him out of the trailer, he won't come."

"What about Pauline? She could just give him a shove with her nose."

"She's not there anymore. Emma unloaded her right away and put her in a little corral inside a different building." Alice tilted her head. "Pauline told me to try stomping and hissing at him, but that didn't work for me

—probably because I'm not nearly as big as she is. I tried sweet-talking, but he's too panicked to listen. He even ignored my claws when I flashed them around." She looked down. "Not that I'd want to claw him anyway."

I huffed. I wouldn't have any problem giving the guy a swipe to get him out the door. "Pauline should've told the bowsers to come along. They could've given him another ride."

"She wouldn't have been able to keep them quiet long enough to avoid being noticed."

I huffed again. "Too bad we can't communicate with Robin or Emma to ask for help."

There was a clanking sound near my carrier. I whipped my head around and realized it was only Pearl butting her food dish against the side of their carrier. When she saw that I was watching, she leaned her front legs against the carrier's slats. "I have an idea!" she chittered.

Great. Another rodent idea. It seemed as if their ideas were only getting me deeper and deeper into trouble.

"What's that?" Alice asked. She shifted toward their carrier.

"Alice—" I started.

"We know what Briggston is afraid of!" squeaked Pearl.

Posha joined Pearl. "Yeah, we know what'll get him running."

Visions of skunks or coyotes or The Vet played

through my head. All well and good—if we'd brought any of those things along. "But—"

"What's that?" Alice interrupted.

"Snakes!" both of the pigs squealed.

My head shot up. "He's scared of snakes?"

Pearl danced about, sending wood chips spewing out of the carrier. "He's so scared of snakes, he won't go anywhere near Bobby's cage. And if Briggston sees one of the kids take Bobby out of his cage at story time, he runs and hides behind Robin's desk."

Well. Of all things, we *had* brought a snake. But how to get Bobby all the way to the trailer without being seen? There were far too many humans in the room.

"What do you think?" I asked Alice.

Her eyes narrowed. "I don't know. I was able to sneak through the door and under the tables without much attention. I look like I belong here. But a snake…"

"I know, I know." When humans spotted a snake, they usually made a lot of fuss. Except for Emma, and Emma wasn't here right now. "Psst, Bob!"

He poked his head out of the bag. "Yessss?"

"Look over there." I tried to poke my paw through the slats to point toward the door, but it wouldn't go through. I nodded in its direction instead.

Bobby swiveled his head. "Yessss?"

"You need to follow Alice under the tables and through that door without being seen. Alice is going to take you with her to scare Briggston out of the trailer. And once you get into the trailer, you *stay* there." No need to chance more human commotion. "Do you think you can do that?"

Bobby stared at the door.

All at once a very loud human voice boomed across the room. "Okay, folks. It's just about time for the judging. Get your pets ready."

The humans had been talking in small groups here and there, but now they began to scatter. I could see Robin coming toward us.

"It's now or never!" I hissed to the snake. "You've got to get out of here. Pronto!"

Bobby kept staring at the door. "I don't think I've ever crawled that far. I don't think I can do it."

"It's that or stay in a cage for the rest of your life. If you want to be free, you've got to take some risks."

My pep talk didn't seem to be helping. Bobby Scales had frozen in place, head sticking out of the bag—in plain sight. Robin was coming closer and closer, heading straight for her bag. Any second now she would see him. She'd catch him and put him into her car, then Briggston would stay in the trailer and I'd stay locked in my cage. I'd end up being the library cat forever!

My claws unsheathed but I couldn't reach Bobby to give him a swipe of encouragement. What was I going to do???

21

A MAD DASH FOR FREEDOM

Rats! Double rats! Triple rats! I wanted to yowl at Bobby, to tell him to *get moving*, but that would make Robin come faster, and I didn't want that. I stood on tiptoe and thrust my nose through the wire of the carrier door. "Alice," I hissed. "Give him a swat with your claws!"

Just then, some terrible squeaks and squeals split the air. I jumped, bonked my head on the top of the carrier, then bumped my nose on the wire as I came back down. Ignoring the ringing in my ears, I scrambled to my feet with claws extended, ready to defend—well, whatever needed defending.

Robin's gaze shifted from her bag to the guinea pigs. "What's the matter, girls?" She stopped beside their carrier and opened the door, reaching inside to pet them.

"Now!" Alice gave Bobby a push with her paw.

Startled, he swayed a bit, then finally started slithering out of the bag. He hesitated just a whisker twitch at the table's edge before beginning to slip down its leg.

"Go, go, go!" I whispered.

Robin gave the pigs a final pat. "Calm down, girls," she was saying. "Don't get too excited or Briggs won't let you on his back."

Bobby's head was on ground level now, then more of his body, and more, and... Robin picked up her bag just as the snake's tail disappeared completely under the table.

By now I was quivering like a leaf in the breeze. Maybe I shouldn't take a chance on Bobby making it to the trailer. Maybe I should make a break for it as soon as Robin opened my carrier. If Alice and I ditched the snake, we could surely make it out of the building without being caught.

Then I thought about Bobby trapped inside a building of hostile humans, and Briggston cowering in Pauline's trailer scared out of his mind, and the pack of library kids who'd be horribly disappointed if their rodent cowgirls didn't have a horse. Not to mention Robin, who'd be sick with worry over her missing cat. And the guinea pigs who'd be upset that they lost their chance at a first place ribbon.

I grimaced. No, I had to stick around to make sure that the snake got to the trailer safely and that Robin found Briggston so he could return to the library where he belonged.

Duty and responsibility—they were both pretty exasperating sometimes.

I gave a full body shake, sheathed my claws, and waited. My whiskers were going positively stiff as boards with the effort of remaining calm.

Robin dug through her bag, pulling out costumes. Soon a couple of kids from story time joined her. Robin handed them the costumes then lifted Posha and Pearl out of their carrier. The kids started dressing the pigs while Robin turned to me.

"I don't know, Briggs." She put her hands on her hips. "You're looking pretty frazzled. Maybe we should just dress the guinea pigs and leave you where you are. You might try to take off on me."

She was too good at reading my mind—except when I was trying to tell her that I wasn't Briggston, that is. I took a deep breath and started purring and rubbing against the cage door. With all the hubbub around us, I had to increase the volume until I could feel my purr vibrating through the entire carrier.

Robin shook her head. "I'd swear you can understand me."

I resisted the urge to lay back my ears. Humans think they're so smart.

Robin finally reached down and unlatched the carrier door. "Okay, we'll do this as planned. But behave yourself. Remember, you're representing the kids at the library."

One of the kids was standing next to my carrier with

the stringy horse tail and blanket in her hands. "You'll be great, Briggston!" she said. Her fingers flexed, and I could imagine them wrapped tight around my belly.

No way! my instincts were screaming.

Duty is duty, duty is duty, my brain was repeating.

My brain won the argument and I let the kid wrap her hands around me and pull me out. She started to attach the swishy hair and blanket. I kept my eye on the door the whole time. I couldn't see Alice or Bobby anymore, so I figured they were sneaking around under the tables. But between the last table and the door was a big empty space they'd have to cross, and that space was even more empty now that the groups of noisy people had all gone back to their pets.

Then a slight movement under the table closest to the door caught my eye. I held my breath as Bobby and Alice crept out from underneath. They headed straight to the nearest wall and reached it without any human cries of alarm. I was beginning to go blue from lack of air, but I couldn't bring myself to breathe yet. Bobby was slithering as fast as he could go along the wall, and Alice was trotting right beside him, probably trying to hide him from view. The snake was a lot longer than Alice, though, and his head and tail were in plain sight.

My tail began to flick, which set my horse tail to flicking, too. Between the itchy blanket, the twitchy horse tail, and my frayed nerves, I felt a little like one of those rubber bands that Emma's nephew likes to play with. The more he stretches them, the harder they snap. That was me. About ready to snap.

Robin must've noticed. She put a hand on my head and started rubbing until I was forced to breathe again. "Don't put the guinea pigs on Briggston until it's almost our turn," she told the kids. "I don't want him giving them a real ride."

Until it's our turn for what? I tore my gaze from the door and looked around the room. Two humans were moving down the line of tables, looking at each animal and talking with its human. They were still a few tables away from us, though.

Suddenly, a shriek split the air. I whipped my head around to see a little kid fleeing across that large open space. Bobby and Alice were hightailing it in the opposite direction, racing for the door that had just been opened by two outgoing humans.

"Snake! Snake!" the kid yelled, and the two humans at the door turned to look. So did all the other humans in the room.

It didn't take long for everyone to spot Bobby. Some of the other kids in the room started screaming, too, and a few squirmed up onto the tables next to their pets. Not the kids from the library, though. The girl who was holding me started shouting. "It's Bobby Scales. Don't hurt him. It's Bobby Scales!"

That got Robin's attention. Someone had started

toward Bobby with a big broom, but Robin yelled, "Don't hurt him. He's the library snake!"

As if by magic, more kids that I recognized appeared from the maze of tables and started running toward the snake. "It's Bobby Scales. It's Bobby Scales!"

"Close the door!" Robin shouted. One of the humans standing there started to do so, but Alice skidded through the opening and stood, half in and half out. Now they couldn't close the door without shutting it on her.

"Get out of the way, cat." The human bent to scoot her out of the way, but Bobby finally reached the door and started slithering outside. The human grabbed Alice then paused, like he couldn't quite bring himself to touch the snake. Alice hissed in his face, which startled the human so that he jerked and let her go. She took off after Bobby, whose tail was just clearing the door.

"Bobby, come back!" cried one of the library kids.

Robin was sprinting for the door now, and she was much faster than the snake. I started wiggling and squirming, forcing the girl who was holding me to loosen her grip. Then I yowled the loudest yowl I'd ever yowled. It was so loud that the kid standing next to Posha and Pearl clapped her hands over her ears.

Robin stopped and turned. I made sure she saw me before I leaped to the floor and tore off through the alleyway of tables. "Briggston!" The girl who'd been holding me started to give chase, but then Posha and Pearl started squeaking and running in circles like they might disappear, too, and both the library kids had to stop and hold onto them instead.

With all of our yowling and squealing and shouting, the other animals in the room were getting pretty nervous. Some of the dogs started yapping, and in a moment, they were joined by a variety of other squeaks, squawks, and howls. The din was so loud I wished *I* had hands to clap over my ears. The humans quickly forgot about Bobby and turned back to their own animals.

Two of the library kids had run outside, and another human was standing in the doorway looking after them. I dashed toward that open door. Now that I was loose, freedom was calling too loudly to be ignored. I wasn't going to stop.

Escape was just a whisker twitch away...

22

SEEING DOUBLE

Unfortunately, Robin suddenly stepped between me and my escape route. "Shut the door!" she shouted, lunging at me.

The human standing in the doorway moved quickly and slammed the door shut when I was just one leap away. I skidded to a stop, but before I could change direction I felt Robin grab me around my middle and lift me into the air, putting an abrupt end to my jailbreak attempt. I started squirming and yowling, but Robin hugged me tightly enough that I didn't have much chance to get loose.

"Poor Briggs," she crooned. "Poor kitty. So scared of snakes. So scared of snakes."

Well, at least I had an excuse for my flight. I could only hope that Alice and Bobby had made a clean getaway.

I allowed Robin to carry me back to the table where

the two kids were still holding Posha and Pearl. "Who brought Bobby Scales?" Her voice had the same edge as Emma's the time she'd left her sandwich on the porch to go answer the phone and had come back to find it missing. (Emma makes yummy sandwiches, by the way.)

The kids looked at each other and back at her. "Dunno," one of them said. "Not me," said the other.

Robin scanned the room, probably searching for some of the other library kids. Then she sighed. "What am I thinking? None of you were at the library this morning and I'm sure Bobby was in his cage when I was getting Posha and Pearl ready. Maybe that wasn't him after all."

The room had started to quiet down.

"Let's put Briggston back together," Robin said. "The judges are starting up again."

They readjusted my itchy blanket, and Robin kept a firm hold on me until the pair of humans Robin had called judges reached our table. The kids put the guinea pigs on top of me, and I felt myself going a little swaybacked.

"You need to go on a diet," I whispered to Posha, who was closest to my shoulder.

"Ditto," the rodent said. "I can barely get my legs around your stomach."

I laid back my ears. "Your legs are too *short*, that's why—"

"Be quiet," Pearl snapped, clicking her teeth at me.

"Remember your responsibility. Concentrate on looking like a horse."

I flicked my tail, but held my ears upright and tried to look like a proper horse. I would be responsible, after all, even if the humiliation of it killed me.

One of the judges had a little box that she pointed in our direction. "Smile for the picture," she said. A light flashed in my eyes and I tensed. But Robin's grip kept me from jumping off the table.

Then the judges asked the kids a bunch of questions, but I didn't pay much attention to how they answered. I kept my eye on the closed door across the room. Even if Bobby managed to roust Briggston out of the trailer, how would Alice get the cat into a building that'd been sealed shut?

The judges finally moved on to look at the bunny in the next carrier, and the library kids took the guinea pigs off my back.

"Good job, Briggston." One of the kids petted me after taking off my itchy blanket. "Way to look like a horse!"

The other kid was removing the costumes from Posha and Pearl. "I think they liked the costumes. Maybe you three will be the winners."

As soon as she put the guinea pigs back into their carrier, they began to jump around like extra large grasshoppers. "Winners, winners," they squeaked.

Robin untangled the swishy, fake tail from my behind

and gave me a good rub down. "I'm so proud of you, Briggs. You've really become an 'out and about' kind of cat lately."

Wait till she got the real Briggston back. Well, I *hoped* she got the real Briggston back. The door, my only escape route, was still firmly closed, and now Robin was getting ready to put me back in the carrier. If I got trapped in there before Alice and Briggston arrived—*if* they arrived—there'd be no chance left to make the switch.

"Do something. Quick!" I hissed at the guinea pigs, who were still hopping and bobbing around in their carrier.

Posha paused. "What?"

"Squeak. Squeal. Do something to distract Robin."

Posha and Pearl looked at each other.

"Quick!" I said again. Robin picked me up and held me tight against her while she opened the carrier door with her free hand.

Suddenly Pearl let out a piercing squeak. Robin turned to look and loosened her grip just a little.

And I was ready. I squirmed free and landed on the floor with all four feet. The impact of my stick foot hitting the ground was enough to rattle my brain, but I didn't let that stop me. I dodged under the table and out of Robin's reach.

"Briggston!" She crouched beside the table, trying to grab me. "Come back here."

No way. I'd never have another chance. I dashed to the

neighboring table and slid underneath. The judges had already left. I figured they were done. Maybe the door would open now.

Robin was suddenly there, swiping at me, but I slid away again. Then one of the library kids crawled under the table and reached for me. Rats! I'd forgotten how nimble kids could be.

I dashed to another table, and another, dodging human feet and trying to avoid the hands reaching down to catch me. I smashed against a carrier that was sitting on the floor, and the mouse inside jumped and squeaked like it was having a heart attack.

While I had my eye on the mouse, feeling a little bummed that I couldn't stick around for my own game of chase, my momentum propelled me straight into a dog sitting under the next table. *Oof!*

I looked up, and the very big, very slobbery canine opened his droopy jowls to show some massive teeth. I thought I was a goner. Then he said, "Woof!" Just once, but I almost fell over from the shock of it.

Robin had caught up and was now looming above me. I scrambled to regain my footing before heading in the opposite direction. Good grief. When was that door going to open?

"Excuse me. Pardon me. Could you please try to grab that cat?" Robin's voice trailed behind me. How long could I keep up with this game of chase? My stick leg was definitely slowing me down, and I was running out of breath trying to drag it around. I needed to get near enough to the door so that I could dash out once it opened, but I also needed to stay far enough away that Robin wouldn't be shouting at the other humans to keep it closed.

I wiggled my way through more feet and slid under yet another table. Unfortunately, I was heading further from the door instead of closer. Another library kid poked his head under the table and grabbed for me. He caught hold of a hind leg, but I hissed and swiped at him with my front claws. He immediately let go.

Great. Now the kids would be terrified of me—uh, Briggston. Whichever of us ended up back at the library.

I slid out from under my current table and—there were no tables left to dodge underneath! I was at the very back of the building now, crouched beside an open space that ran along the last row of tables. The space was wide enough for humans to walk back and forth, but not much bigger. A few humans were standing in the middle of that narrow space holding leashes attached to large dogs, and both humans and dogs were staring at me.

Obviously not a good place to stay. I did an about face, but there was that kid again, crawling further under the table to grab me. I skidded away, but now I was completely out in the open. Not much room to maneuver, especially with my clumsy leg. I tried to dodge the kid, but then Robin appeared from the other side.

Only one way left to run. I headed for the back corner,

even though my brain was screaming, "This is a trap!" I clamped down my ears and forced myself to sprint faster. I was going to stay out of a human's grasp as long as possible.

Suddenly a rush of fresh air smacked against my face, and a thin crack in the wall magically widened into an opening—a back door!

I leaped for this new escape route, my legs extending in midair, when suddenly a furry orange object crossed my flight path. I crashed into it and went down in a tangle of limbs—and there were a lot of limbs. Too many to be just my own, although they all certainly looked like mine. In fact, I could swear I was seeing double—even down to the two stick legs that kept tripping me when I was trying to scrabble back to my feet. Maybe the crash had muddled my vision.

Before I could regain my balance, Robin dashed around a table and grabbed me. At exactly the same time, another pair of hands grabbed the orange feline that'd been tangled up with me. We were both hefted into the air.

I squeezed my eyes shut, hoping to get rid of the double images, and when I opened them again, my twin was gone. *Whew!*

Instead, a black cat had appeared below me.

Alice! My jaw dropped and my entire body went limp.

"George, are you okay?"

That was Emma's voice! I twisted to look at the human holding me, but it was Robin.

I swiped my paw over my eyes. I really *had* hit my head too hard.

But then I turned back—and there was Emma! She was holding another orange cat who seemed to be me, but couldn't be me since I was over here, and she was staring at me—the me currently being held by Robin, that is.

Robin hugged me even more tightly. "Uh, hi. Is that your cat?"

"I thought so." Emma looked down at the cat she was holding. "He's the cat I chased into the building, at least. Is that your cat?" She nodded toward me.

Robin looked down at me. "He's the cat I brought to the pet show, and I *thought* he was mine, but now…" Her voice trailed off.

"They look exactly the same." Emma turned Briggston toward her. He'd gone limp and glassy-eyed, like he'd been terrorized by a pack of coyotes and was just now realizing that he was still alive. "Except," Emma continued, "their casts are on different legs."

She and Robin looked at each other. Suddenly Robin gasped. "Did you have your cat at the vet clinic last Tuesday?"

"Yes." Emma narrowed her eyes, like she does when she's puzzling out how to get a stray sheep back into the corral. "Did you?"

"Yes." Robin's voice rose, and her grip got tighter.

"When I picked Briggs up from the vet, I thought his cast was on the wrong leg, but the tag on the cage said it was him."

"George has been acting strange all week," said Emma. "He's been hiding inside the house. Acting terrified around the other animals."

"And Briggs' behavior has been odd, too." Robin looked down at me again, and her eyes opened wide. "We had the wrong cats!" She untucked me from under her arm and looked me straight in the eye. "You aren't Briggston, are you?"

I reached out to pat her face with my good paw.

She gave me a hug, then set me gently on the floor. "Sorry about that, cat," she said, rubbing my back. "I'll bet you want to go home."

You could say that again. I stumbled over to Emma, and Alice met me. She started licking my ears so enthusiastically that I could almost feel my fur detaching.

Emma set Briggston on the ground, too. He collapsed, then staggered to his feet and wobbled over to Robin.

"They definitely know to whom they belong," Robin said. She picked up Briggston. "Poor cat. He's terrified of being outdoors, you know."

"And George doesn't like being trapped inside." Emma looked down at me, but didn't try to pick me up. She evidently trusted me to come with her. What a relief to be back with a human who understood me! "Sorry about the mix up," Emma said.

Robin nodded. "Me, too."

A pack of kids had gathered around Robin, listening to the exchange with wide eyes. One of them pointed at me. "That's not Briggston?"

"Nope." Robin crouched down, like she was talking to me instead of the other humans. "But he's welcome to come back and visit us at the library any time. We couldn't have done the costume contest without him."

Briggston shook himself. His eyes were clearing. "Home!" he said, although I'm sure Robin thought he was just purring.

Robin stood. "Okay, kids. Let's get everything packed up."

Briggston looked over Robin's shoulder at me as they walked away. "Thanks."

And it was the best thing I'd heard in a long, long time.

23

WHEN A PLAN COMES TOGETHER

Emma let me walk to the trailer on my own. She even let me crawl into the trailer with Alice instead of insisting that the two of us ride in the cab of the pickup with her. After she'd left to fetch Pauline, Alice and I padded to the back and sat on some loose hay. I almost jumped straight to the ceiling, though, when suddenly Bobby's head popped out in front of me.

"Bobby Scales!" I'd almost forgotten about him in the hubbub. "You got away!"

"Thankssss to you," he said, weaving back and forth.

I turned and looked at Alice to keep from getting dizzy. "So tell me what happened after the two of you got out of the door. I've obviously missed something."

Alice's ears twitched, and she sprawled on the hay. "It's been a bugger of a day, hasn't it, Bob?"

The snake nodded and put his head back down. "We jusssst barely esssscaped with our livessss."

Alice started licking her shoulder, but I nudged her out of the way. "You talk, I'll lick."

"Well," said Alice, leaning into me, "we got out of the building, but there were humans after us, you know."

I nodded, but kept licking.

"Luckily, there was some tall grass around the side of the building, and we dashed into that. The humans couldn't find us right away, so they gave up. We hid there for a little while to make sure no one was still on the look-out, then snuck over to Emma's trailer."

I stopped licking. "You snuck a snake through a bunch of humans?"

Alice nodded. "It wasn't too hard, actually. We slipped from building to building, sticking to the edges and crossing the open spaces at the back where there weren't so many humans. We made it without being seen." She tilted her head as though she was feeling pretty proud of herself.

I was proud of her, too. "Great job, Alice. With your smarts, you should be chief in charge of security for this entire town."

Her eyes glinted. "And I could do it, too."

I looked over at Bobby. "So you must've been able to scare Briggston out of the trailer."

"Eassssy-peasssssy," the snake said. "All I did was

sssstare at him, and he sssskedaddled as fasssst as he could go."

"The problem," Alice continued, "was stopping him from running in a blind panic. I practically had to tackle him to get him to listen to me. I finally dragged him over to a grassy patch and convinced him to do some deep breathing."

I scratched my ears. "And how did you get Emma to follow you? That was the cleverest thing yet. I'd never have thought to bring her along, too."

"Uh…" Alice brushed at her nose. "That wasn't really my idea. She was walking back to the trailer when she saw us sneaking out of the grass, heading toward your building. She shouted at us to stop, but of course we didn't. So she gave chase. I figured we were goners when we got to the door of your building and it was closed. But Bobby and I had been at the back of the building on our way to the trailer, and I remembered there'd been a door there, too, and it'd been propped open just a crack. So we dashed around to the back, and I had just enough time to paw open the door before Emma reached us."

Whew. Alice was out of breath from telling the story, and I was out of breath from hearing it. "I can't believe it actually worked," I said. "After Robin caught me, I figured I was destined to be a library cat for the rest of my life."

"I was getting pretty worried, too," said Alice. "If we hadn't been able to open the door, Emma would've had us for sure. And then Briggston would've been a farm cat forever, whether he liked it or not."

"And now I get to be a farm sssnake!" said Bobby, rearing up again. "When can I sssstart?"

I butted his head with mine. "Let's get home first," I said. "And I'll introduce you to the troops. Then we'll need to find a place for you to hole up for the winter. And I'll need to do a full report with Pauline, and we'll have to figure out a way to spring Kid from the pen again, and I'm sure that Aunt Eloise is up to her neck in mice, and—"

Alice tackled me and rolled me on my side. Pretty easy to do with my stick leg throwing me off balance. "There'll be plenty of time after we get home," she said. "Now can we take a nap? I'm just exhausted!"

So we curled up together, two cats and a snake, and slept all the way home.

24

HAPPY HOMECOMING

I sat outside the corral that evening listening to Pauline's report. She didn't have much to say, of course, since she'd been at the fair all day. With Pauline gone, the sheep had been stuck in the corral, and they were shuffling and snuffling and bleating in complaint. But that didn't bother Pauline—or Felix or Kid, who were sitting with me.

Pauline glanced at the sheep to make sure they weren't getting into trouble, then leaned down and whuffled Kid with her nose. "Glad to be out of the pen again?"

"Glad! Glad!" Kid flapped her little wings and bounced up and down. I was amazed how much her speech had improved in the week I'd been gone. She was only a couple months old, but she was definitely a fast learner. She'd been so happy to see me when I came home that she'd beat her wings, sprinted around the pen (well, waddled), and tried to fly, making such a ruckus that Emma had wisely let her out. No need for the chicks to work themselves into a frenzy, too.

"More like ecstatic," said Felix. "And that makes two of us." He was sprawled out on a patch of grass that was far enough from the corral to have escaped the attention of the sheep.

I stared at him. "Really? I figured you'd like having me out of the way. No more being ordered around and all that."

Felix tilted his head and batted a fly that was dive-bombing his ears. "Wasn't as fun as I thought it would be. Too much responsibility. Aunt Eloise complained about mice, Kid complained about being locked up, Pauline complained about gophers, the dogs complained about Old Mangy eating their food, Emma complained about birds eating her raspberries in the garden—" He yawned. "Even Lil complained because I wasn't hanging around the porch enough."

His tail twitched and he closed his eyes, leaning back into the waning sunlight. "Now that you're back, you can take the guff again."

"Uh, thanks—I think." I didn't know if that meant he was willing to let me order him around now, or if he was planning on curling up on his porch and never setting foot in the farmyard again. But I didn't want to open that can of worms tonight. Tonight everyone was happy to see me, and I didn't want to ruin the mood.

"You told the snake to stay out of the corral, right?" Pauline was studying the sheep who'd clustered in one corner of the corral with their noses pushed together like they were either gossiping or plotting a revolt.

"Yeah. He's perfectly happy to stay in the barn and practice his mouse hunting technique. I don't know if Aunt Eloise is happy about his company or not, but she certainly can't complain about the extra help. Especially someone who's *willing* to help." I narrowed my eyes at Felix but he just twitched his tail, ignoring me.

Kid prodded my side with her bill. "I help."

I butted her with my head. "I know. You're perfect help. But stay away from Bobby, okay? You're not much bigger than a mouse right now, and I don't want him mistaking you for supper. We'll find him a comfy hole in the pasture for hibernating this winter, and by spring you'll have grown enough that he won't be interested."

Kid flapped her wings and settled next to me, bill across my back. We rested in silence for a bit while watching the colors of the sunset spread across the sky.

I finally nudged Kid out of the way and stood, giving myself a fur-flying shake. "Okay, troops, better call it a night. Tomorrow will be busy." Kid waddled at my side as I padded back to my own bed in my own garage.

It was good to be home.

EPILOGUE

I sat in the pet carrier at The Vet's, swishing my tail and staring through the bars of the latched door. Emma had come to the garage bright and early this morning, lured me into her car with talk of visiting Alice and Twila, then stopped here instead. She'd promised that we'd only stay long enough for The Vet to check my leg to be sure I hadn't hurt it again while making my escape attempt at the fair, and afterwards we'd head straight to Twila's. If she hadn't promised that, I would've yowled and scratched and refused to let her put me in the carrier, which she'd conveniently pulled out of the car's trunk.

Still, I was keeping the room under surveillance, just in case The Vet had different ideas—and also in case the giant dog sitting across from me suddenly decided he wanted a cat snack. A Great Dane, Emma had called him when she'd been talking with the dog's human. Nothing "great" about that long-legged canine, I figured, except seeing his tail as he walked out the door. I didn't like the way he was eyeballing me.

Emma was in a chair next to me, holding a newspaper and staring at it. Because of my experience at the library, I knew she must be doing that thing called reading. But I wished she was keeping an eye on the Not-So-Great Dane dog instead. One snap of his jaws, and I'd be a goner.

The Vet was taking an awfully long time. I stretched one way and then another, trying to get comfortable in the cramped space.

"Listen to this, George." Emma's voice interrupted my squirming. "The headline reads 'Cat Steals the Show.'"

I pricked my ears and thought about the pet show I'd attended with the guinea pigs and Bobby Scales. What would a cat want to steal at that place? Kitty treats maybe?

"Look, here's the picture." Emma held the paper close to the carrier for me to see.

I peered through the bars and my fur instantly poofed. The paper showed a flat cat wearing a stringy mane and tail and carrying two flat guinea pig cowgirls on his back.

"That's you, George." Emma laughed.

I stared. It sure looked like me, and the guinea pigs were exact copies of Posha and Pearl. But how could I be flattened in the newspaper and sitting in the pet carrier at the same time? My mind started whirling. Could the picture, as Emma had called it, only be a copy of us and not the real thing?

Picture...picture... I'd heard that word several times at the library when looking at flattened animals, but I'd also heard it somewhere else. Somewhere...

My ears shot up as I suddenly remembered. The judge at the fair had pointed her little box at us and said, "Smile for the picture."

That's it! She'd done something with her box that'd made a copy of me and the guinea pigs. We hadn't been flattened—we'd been copied. That meant the books in the library weren't full of flattened animals and people—just *copies* of animals and people!

My mind was zinging and my fur tingling with this revelation. I hadn't felt this excited since Aunt Eloise had retired and officially promoted me to chief in charge of farm security. If learning about reading was this much fun, maybe I should also be trying to figure out how squiggles turned into letters to make words.

I leaned closer to watch as Emma continued reading. "'A cat and two guinea pigs were the winning entry in the small animal dress-up contest at the county fair on Tuesday. The three animals all supposedly belonged to the town library. It was discovered after the show, however, that the cat had only been masquerading as the library cat. He and Briggston, the true library cat, had been accidentally switched at the veterinarian's clinic several days before. The two cats happened upon each other at the fair in an encounter that must've been coincidence, but almost seemed orchestrated by the animals themselves.'"

Emma set the paper aside and laughed again. "That reporter has a good sense of humor, George. He thinks you and Briggston arranged to meet at the fair."

I narrowed my eyes. Little did she know.

She looked down at me. "I'm glad Briggston decided to sneak to the fair with Pauline, though, or I might never have figured out why you'd suddenly become so intent on being a house cat. I missed having you pattering around the farmyard and skulking through the garden. I even missed having you underfoot."

Underfoot? I was only underfoot when Emma's big, clumsy feet got in the way. Crazy human. But I was glad she'd missed me, just like I'd missed her and all my animal friends on the farm.

I tilted my head, just realizing something important. Posha and Pearl were my friends now, too, along with a bunch of library kids who liked to read books and pet me. And Robin, who'd said I could come back and visit any time.

It suddenly struck me that I was *glad* I'd been mistaken for Briggston. I'd been frustrated, true, but I'd learned a lot while I was there, and I was ready to learn more. I definitely wanted to find out how to turn squiggles into words.

"Your turn, George." The Assistant was standing at an open door, motioning to Emma.

Emma lifted my carrier and headed toward the room.

"Let's get that leg checked out, George, so you can get back to chasing mice without any more complications."

That's right. I was ready to get back to work. I had a duckling, a reluctant grey cat, and a new snake recruit to train for farm patrol duties. I had two distractible canines, a flock of feather-brained chickens, and a kibble-eating coyote to whip into shape. And I also had to return to the library for a visit so the guinea pigs could teach me to read.

Felix was right: being in charge of security came with a lot of responsibility. But I was up to the challenge. Watch out mice, watch out Mangy, watch out whatever other problem may come my way. Chief George was back, and ready for action!

ACKNOWLEDGMENTS

There's an old saying, "it takes a village to raise a child." The same is true for the making of a book, and I've been blessed with many helpful "villagers" for the creation of this one. The nearest and dearest of course are my husband, Kris, and children, Miriam and Isaac. They are always willing to play the role of George and "converse" in his voice to help me brainstorm his adventures. They've assisted me in coming up with enough crazy situations that George will be hard pressed to experience them all!

Also much appreciation goes to my writing sisters, Rebecca Johnson, Val Padmore, and Beth Summers, who patiently read every draft, asked questions, and truthfully told me what they thought. You three are everything I could hope for in a writing group! Thanks also to my publisher at Prairieland Press, Nancy Wagner, for her incredible energy and patience, to my editor, Rebecca Johnson, for doing her usual superb work catching details, to Jean Cox and Miriam Ganoung for giving the manuscript a final read through, and to my illustrator, Kathleen Gadeken, for the wonderful drawings of George!

Besides those who helped with the basic creation of the book, I have some special people to acknowledge. First, my uncle, Dr. Donald Dreyer, a small animal veterinarian in Longmont, CO, who was more than happy to talk with me on the telephone about George's injured leg and give me advice on how quickly a cat might be expected to recover. This conversation was made more meaningful because my uncle had been diagnosed with a rare form of cancer earlier in the year and was very weak at the time. It turned out to be the last time I talked with him.

And finally, the library animals in this book were actually named by children, just like Posha mentions in the story— not children from the library, but those whose classrooms I've had the privilege of visiting. I conducted a character naming contest in early 2019 and invited any classroom I'd visited to submit names for consideration. Here are the classrooms with the winning entries:

Briggston was named by Shelly Goldfish's first and second grade class in Elba, Nebraska.

Bobby Scales was a combination of names suggested by Amy Rohe's fifth grade class at the IKM-Manning, Iowa, school district and by Elaine Blum's fifth grade class in Elba, Nebraska.

Posha and Pearl were names chosen by Jeanine Saner's first grade class in Halsey, Nebraska.

Thanks to all of the classrooms that submitted names. This was an exciting part of the writing process and I was so glad to have your participation!

Want to share more adventures with George?

George and the Stolen Sunny Spot

George Trains the Troops

Look for them in your favorite bookstore!

Made in the USA
Middletown, DE
06 April 2021

37130923R00109